The Trails I Walked at the Foot of Ngong Hills

The Trails I Walked at the Foot of Ngong Hills

Dr. Martina Kaumbulu Ebesugawa

Illustrations by Juan J. Marquez Portal

MILLCITY
PRESS

Mill City Press, Inc.
212 3rd Avenue North, Suite 290
Minneapolis, MN 55401
612.455.2294
www.millcitypublishing.com

ISBN-13: 978-1-62652-186-5
LCCN: 2013908388

Printed in the United States of America

Special Thanks to the Lee, Ynes, and Cookman families who helped to make this book possible. Special Gratitude to Kristen Williams and Julia Weinberg for their editorial guidance.

Duane, I could not have done it without you. I love you, Coral!

Dedicated most of all to Life (I Am) for paving a road towards compassion on behalf of mankind.

Dedicated to our ancestors, whose voices are still heard!

CONTENTS

A NOTE FROM THE AUTHOR

The Trails I Walked at the Foot of Ngong Hills is a series of eight vignettes and a monograph for teachers. It opens with a recapitulated Akamba folktale, which sets the tone for the book. The text is a multicultural young readers book. It is told through the life of Bahati, a fictional bi-cultural Mukamba and African American girl and later woman who, through betrothal, becomes a part of the Asian culture. The book is based on accounts from the author's life as a Mukamba and African American person who grew up in Kenya.

Mukamba is singular for Akamba. The Akamba people are a tribe in the eastern province of Kenya. The *Trails I walked at the Foot of Ngong Hills* captures Bahati's experiences in the world as seen from the eyes of a Mukamba person. The Akamba people are known as storytellers. "Every Mukamba is a story-teller, but naturally some people are better than others. Old men and women know a great number of them. One gets the impression that their 'fountain' of stories never dries up," writes Mbiti (1984). This fountain of stories provides the reader with a look into various multicultural themes and a personal multicultural story through Bahati's life experiences as a young girl, adolescent, and woman.

The book begins with a retold Mukamba story, *A Man Who Helped the Needy*. As is traditional, animals are used to represent people, which keeps the confidentiality of the individual hidden from the common listener. By doing this, the parable is told and the life lesson learned. The author uses pseudonyms, instead of animals, that reflect the inner qualities of specific characters in the main text. In doing this, the author tells Bahati's Kamba story. The vignettes that follow are based on authentic cultural experiences of the author. The vignettes describe urban life in Nairobi following independence in the 1970s and 80s, Akamba celebrations, adolescent struggles, multicultural relationships, intergenerational relationships, faith, hope, and love, as told by Bahati.

The monograph that follows the eight vignettes is a scholarly essay, which serves as a justification for this multicultural book.

There are few African children's books written by African authors. *The Trails I Walked at the Foot of Ngong Hills* captures for children everywhere an authentic glimpse into Akamba and Kenyan life. This look into Kenyan life will capture imaginations and inspire all children to tell their personal stories to the world.

The *Trails I Walked at the Foot of Ngong Hills* is written to inspire life's next generation of children to know, respect, and live together in harmony as their Maker intended. It describes the different struggles and rewards people encounter in their multicultural journeys and captures the essence of what Akamba people hold dear: Mulungu, elders, and the human family!

FOREWORD

I have been inspired by Martina Kaumbulu Ebesugawa's determination, intellect, and presence since I happened to meet her one afternoon in her office cubicle. She was working on a research presentation for the Hawaii International Conference on Education, where she was presenting her dissertation findings. I offered to review it for her. She was so accepting and joyous of my offer that we became instant friends.

Over the years since then, she has led me to be more connected to my spiritual life and also to appreciate the hard work of research, the thrill of getting results, and the precision of presenting those results at conferences and in publications.

Martina Kaumbulu Ebesugawa continues to amaze me with this, her latest project, *The Trails I Walked at the Foot of Ngong Hills* for teens and teachers to use in their classrooms. I hope you are as impressed as I am by her prolific work and will enjoy whatever she sets her mind to next.

Lori Wensley, PhD
Alta Bates Medical Staff, Berkeley CA
ChildSolutions, San Leandro, CA

INTRODUCTION

A Man Who Helped the Needy
(An Akamba Folktale Retold)

There is one who is free in giving, and yet he grows richer. And there is one who keeps what he should give, but he ends up needing more. The man who gives much will have much, and he who helps others will be helped himself.

Proverbs 11:24–25 (NLV)

Once upon a long, long time ago there lived a king who had a beautiful daughter. The king loved his daughter and guarded her with his life. As she grew in age, she became more pleasant and lovely in character and appearance. As all Kamba fathers do, the king sought a fitting suitor for his daughter. One day he had the Ngoma played to announce to the kingdom's people that a gathering was going to take place. Once the people had gathered, the king informed the people that he was going to bring his daughter forward to present her to the kingdom, at which time he would present a challenge to all her suitors. The suitor who met his challenge would be given his daughter in marriage.

Now, a humble man who lived in the king's kingdom found out about the king's intentions with his daughter, and set out from his small village to meet the king's challenge. He was not a wealthy man; he had little in his pockets, but he packed his few belongings along with some food and water for the long journey to the king's palace where the princess lived. His belongings consisted of his clothes, fire-making tools, dishes, and food articles including millet, dried fish, goat meat, and water. The distance between his village and the king's palace was great, so he knew that he would have to pace himself for the long journey.

He walked one whole day until the sun began to set and soon night fell. He ate his dinner and went to bed for the night. In the middle of the night he heard some noise among the bushes surrounding him, for he had gone to sleep on the savannah plain. He quickly woke up and lit a fire with his fire-making tools. As the red glow from the fire grew brighter, he could see clearly what looked like a large lion. The man immediately thought about how he was going to defend himself against the lion. But before he could raise his bow and arrow to shoot the lion, it spoke to the man and said, "I am hungry, please don't shoot me. Can you give me something to eat?" The man was baffled that the lion could talk. He listened as the lion spoke again, "Please give me something to eat. If you help me now, I will help you at the proper time." The man was worried about his journey, but he knew all of Mulungu's creatures were important, so he gave the lion some of his meat to eat. The lion thanked him and let the man return to bed without harming him. The next morning the man got up and continued his journey to the palace.

The man walked for several more miles until he felt tired and came to rest under a luscious baobab tree. While he was resting, a swarm of weaverbirds circled the baobab tree under which he was resting. They settled themselves on the tree's branches. The birds were curious, had clear vision, and could see the man's bag of millet on the ground. The birds spoke to the man and said, "Please share your millet with us, we are very hungry and our migrant journey is long. If you help us now, we will help you at the proper time." The man thought, how strange, first the lion and now these weaverbirds! "Weaverbirds, I have little to eat and I am on a long journey. If I give you my food, what will I have to eat?" But the weaverbirds assured the man that they would come through for him when he needed them. So he shared his food with them, then they flew away. After this, he packed his belongings and continued on his journey to the palace.

He travelled for another full day and then stopped to rest. He was now very, very tired and hungry. He felt miserable inside and wondered if it was worth having shared his food with the lion and birds. Yet, while he was feeling miserable under a thorn tree, another set of birds flew up and settled above his head. Now the man thought to himself, "First the lion, then the weaverbirds. What do these pink-backed pelicans want from me?"

"Friend," the birds said, "please give us some of your dried fish." They could see the man's fish on the ground with his fire-making tools and water gourd. "Birds," the man said, "if I give you some of my fish I will have little to eat for my long journey as I have shared my millet and my meat with the weaverbirds and a lion." The birds replied, "Neighbor, if you share your food with us now, we will help you when the time comes." So the man shared his fish with the birds and the birds flew away. Soon he was on his way to the palace.

As he approached the palace, he was still a long distance off but he could hear the drummers drumming for the Mbeni. The young men were dancing with anticipation of marrying the king's daughter. The man was tired and had about half day's journey still to go. He thought, I will drink some of my water to refresh myself and then I will be on my way. As he was about to put the gourd of water to his lips for a drink, he heard buzzing above him. There was a beehive in the tree where he had stopped to drink his water and find refreshment. The bees spoke to him, saying, "Friend, please give us some of your water for we are thirsty from the long drought. We need to carry some of this water off to our children in another beehive, who need water and are dying." The man replied, "Bees, first I should not be talking to insects and animals, for they don't talk, but since you are Mulungu's creatures I will respect that he may have a message for me. But bees, I am trying to get to the palace where I will attempt to overcome the king's challenge and take his daughter's hand in marriage. If I give you the water, I may not have enough strength to get to the palace." But the bees replied, "Friend, if you help us now, we will help you at the appropriate time." So the man shared his water with the bees and they finished the water remaining in his gourd. They thanked him and promised him that he would be honored for his generosity someday.

The man was soon on his way and made it to the palace. When he got there, there were people of every race and culture walking around the palace. The man heard the drums and saw the young men dancing the Mbeni, for they all hoped to wow the princess with their talent. But the king changed his mind and decided not to present his daughter before the people. Instead the king disguised his daughter and had her mingle among the people. The king told the young suitors that the man who could distinguish the princess from the other women would win her hand in marriage. This was a challenging task for the men, for the princess had grown up in the palace separate from other people. No one in the village knew what she looked like except the king and his court.

The people were baffled and began to look for the king's daughter among each other. The humble man was bewildered also, because he was from a village far from the palace court and did not have a clue as to what the princess looked like or who she was in person. Then all of a sudden the man heard buzzing in his ear. He flapped his hand across his ear to get rid of the buzzing, but a bee came back, and it spoke. "It's your friend, the bee. Follow me, I will fly by the princess as though to sting her, and if the young maiden attempts to swat me with her hands and chase me, you will know that she is the princess, the daughter of the king." The bee went on, "Once you see her flap her hands, be brave, oh man, and take her hand and announce to the crowd that she is indeed the king's daughter." Then the bee flew away and the humble man waited until he heard some commotion in the distance, then he saw the most beautiful and noble looking maiden flapping her hands and chasing a bee. The humble man walked over to her to chase the bees away, but tripped and fell on a broken branch in the road. The pink-backed pelicans flew by and helped the man up to his feet. The man lost sight of the bee and the princess in the crowd. Then the weaverbirds told the man not to worry that they would fly over the crowd and find the princess and bee. The birds saw the princess flapping her hands and chasing the bee away. Then the birds went and led the humble man to the princess. Once the bee saw the man, the bee obeyed the man, did not put up a fight, and left the princess. Then the humble man walked over to identify the princess, but another suitor saw the man walking toward the princess. This man was selfish and would do anything to get what he wanted, even harm another suitor. The selfish man was filled with envy and wanted to get to the princess first, so he pushed the humble man down to the ground. The humble man was distraught and the selfish man thought he had won the princess's hand. Suddenly, however, the lion pounced on the selfish man and growled loudly at him. The selfish man had no courage in him as he was selfish and not a true warrior, for it takes selflessness to be a true warrior. The selfish man's heart melted with fear and he ran away from the lion. Then the humble man stood up and took the princess's hand and announced to the crowd and king that she was indeed the king's daughter. The lion growled at the crowd in honor of the humble man, and everyone bowed at his feet. The man's humble appearance and his face, which shone brightly with kindness and warmth, amazed the king. The princess, too, noticed these qualities and in her heart she was at peace that such a man had found her. The king quickly took his daughter's hand and the humble man's hand and announced to the crowd that this humble man would marry his daughter and become king after him, which he did. The man, though humble and poor, shared what he had with others when they were in need, and in his time of need he was refreshed greatly. So as the proverb states, when we honor and refresh others, we ourselves are refreshed. Most importantly, when we refresh others generously we become both noble and distinguished in character and our reward is boundless!

A Story Begins

Perfect love puts fear
out of our hearts!
1John 4:18 (NLV)

Truth and Love, a choice!

Difference knocks; scared, I hide!

Open up, I'm Free!

VIGNETTE NUMBER ONE
My First Neighborhood

Bahati lived in a foreign land far from the Ngong Hills and dreamt often of her home in Lang'ata where she had grown up. Her father and mother had established their family's permanent residence in Lang'ata during her middle childhood, and she could see the Ngong Hills from her bedroom window. Before moving to her family home in Lang'ata, Bahati remembered living and playing with her friends in Moi Estate. Moi Estate was a humble neighborhood in Nairobi, the capital of Kenya. Prior to living in Moi Estate, Bahati lived in the college town across the Atlantic where she was born and her parents attended university. Bahati was in nursery school when she came to live in a small two-bedroom house in Moi Estate. She lived in Moi Estate until she was in Standard 5, and it was a wonderful time in Bahati's life. Bahati's house in Moi Estate was on the right-hand side of the corner as you came up into the neighborhood. Off the main road and close to the barracks, she remembered seeing soldiers dressed neatly in their uniforms. She remembered how clean the barracks looked from the car window when her father drove the family back from the city center. Bahati remembered that the barracks were on the street perpendicular to the road that led up to Bahati's house. Bahati's house had a green roof and was painted white, as were all the houses in this part of Moi Estate. In the years to come, the neighborhood would expand and new two-story homes would be built with red roofs to distinguish them from the old ones. By that time, however, Bahati's family had moved to Lang'ata and lived just off Magadi Road, near Bomas of Kenya and the Nairobi Zoo, where many tourists would come to visit.

Moi Estate, as Bahati remembered it, was a mixture of families and individuals who had returned to Kenya after gaining their college degrees from universities overseas or had moved to Nairobi from the countryside to gain employment. She recalled seeing people from various races in the neighborhood, including East Indians, Caucasians, and Africans from different tribes and countries. Bahati recalled hearing many Kenyan tribal languages, including Luo, Kikuyu, Maasai, and Kikamba, among a few, as she walked down the neighborhood streets, sat in her neighbors' homes, or mingled with people as they bustled around the town's shopping area. She heard also people speaking English and Swahili to each other. She recalled that the East Indian storeowner spoke Swahili and English to her brother and her, whenever they would come in to buy groceries. Almost all Kenyans spoke English and Swahili, the nation's two common languages. These two national languages allowed everyone the opportunity to communicate regardless of race or tribe.

Across the street from Bahati's house in Moi Estate was a family similar to her own. Sabrina lived with her parents and younger sister. Her family was bi-cultural and bi-racial. Sabrina's father was from Trinidad and her mother was a Caucasian American. Sabrina's house had some similarities to Bahati's, as her mother was also American, but Sabrina's home was sparsely furnished and her parents did not seem like they were invested in the neighborhood. Years later, Sabrina's parents separated and Sabrina and her sister stayed with Bahati and her family for a few months. Sabrina and her family later moved to Trinidad. Bahati's mother was very loyal to Bahati's father and she made a home for them wherever they lived. Bahati noticed that this was the difference between the two families. Bahati's family was here to stay, while Sabrina's was just passing through Moi Estate and later Kenya itself.

Next to Sabrina lived Wamai's family. They were Kikuyu and from a different tribe than Bahati's father, who was a Mukamba. Wamai and his family ate different uji from Bahati's and her other friends. Wamai's family used millet to make their uji in the morning and Bahati's family used white maize meal from the store down the street. Bahati loved to visit her friends and neighbors. Each of them was different from the other, and the cultural practices they had in their homes resembled their heritage.

Bahati's favorite friend in the neighborhood was Wanjiko. She lived up the street and to the left of Bahati. Wanjiko had light brown skin and a pleasant personality. Bahati and Wanjiko played doctor almost every day and would make a mess at Wanjiko's house. Bahati and Wanjiko's nannies would get angry with them. "Wanjiko and Bahati! You have spilled so much water on the floor. Who is going to clean it up?" they would ask. Bahati and Wanjiko were just happy to be together. Both girls wanted to be doctors when they grew up and would pretend to deliver babies when they played together. Wanjiko was one of Bahati's best friends. Wanjiko was temperate and kind and not easily troubled. Bahati, on the other hand, struggled with anxiety and often wanted to get away from home, where it was sometimes turbulent. Bahati remembered the peace she felt playing with Wanjiko every afternoon. Wanjiko was a loyal friend as well. During adolescence, Bahati had struggled to find as loyal and close a friend as Wanjiko. As the days, weeks, months, and years passed, Bahati would often think back to her time at Moi Estate with Wanjiko. Her memories of childhood warmed her heart and reminded her that people could be good and kind inside.

Bahati had a few friends, neighbors, and others whom she was fond of, while she lived in Moi Estate. Prinina and Wanjiko were two. Prinina was a beautiful Ugandan woman with dark brown skin, short hair, and a brilliant smile. Prinina was Bahati's caregiver while Bahati's parents were at work. Bahati and her family loved Prinina; she was a kind and loving woman who had a gentle and loving spirit. Bahati and her siblings enjoyed eating Prinina's meals. Prinina was from Kampala in Uganda and had different recipes from Bahati's Akamba aunties and African American mother. She made matoke, sukama wiki, and fish. For dessert, Bahati would enjoy a common East African dessert, maziwa lala and ugali. Bahati preferred to have fresh milk on her ugali rather than curds, or maziwa lala. After lunch Bahati and her siblings would go out to play with their friends in the neighborhood.

House workers like Prinina and Florence, Wanjiko's caregiver, were common in Kenya. After Jamuri, independence, in 1963, many house workers who had served the British colonialists were left without jobs when their employers returned to England. Many of these workers sought employment from fellow Kenyans regardless of race. Kenyans were representative of various races, including African, East Indian, and European (mostly former British citizens). Philip and Richard Leaky, sons of famed British archeologists Louis and Mary Leaky, are examples of European Kenyans. They were very active in Kenyan society and even became government officials. Many government officials, businessmen, and other professionals employed these workers and built homes for them. House workers were employed and treated well, if the house owner could afford it. Many of the house workers who were employed in Moi Estate lived in Kibera and would walk to work every day. Prinina lived in Kibera, because Bahati's parents rented their home and could not afford to house her. Bahati's mother, however, went out of her way to ensure that Prinina had what she needed to live as well as she could.

As an adult, Bahati learned that her father had been a houseboy before he had gone to university in the United States of America. Bahati could see why her father cherished life and respected the working-class man. He spent much of his life trying to support and empower various individuals to a better life. He did this because he lived their lives and understood the struggles of being poor, a servant, and an Ambua man living in a colonized country. Despite this, he was able to rise above the boxes that life had set out for him to live in, ultimately becoming a wealthy and generous landowner.

He was able to live his life and advocate for the voices of the people least heard in society. At his funeral, hundreds of people of all races came to honor him; it was a testimony to his dedication to humanity.

Kenya had received its Uhuru, freedom, from the British and now it was fifteen years later. Africans were hirable in positions they had not been in the past and could afford a decent living. Despite independence, Kenya struggled with its segregation and prejudices among the peoples living in the country. Some prejudices were based on race, while others on social economic status and tribal differences. Bahati noticed that a lot of older Caucasian people and their families lived in Karen, a suburb in Nairobi. Later, Bahati learned that most of the Caucasian people who lived in Karen were pre-colonial landowners who did not leave after independence in 1963. Newer expatriates from Europe and India lived in Westlands, Lavington, and a few in Karen too. Most African Kenyans lived in various parts of Nairobi including Moi Estate, Madaraka, and Dakorete Corner. The wealthier African Kenyans lived alongside the British, East Indians, and expatriates in Westlands, Lavington, and Karen. Bahati recalled that the homes in these areas were huge, many mansions built on large acres of land. It was a stark comparison to the people who lived in tin roofed homes built close together in Kibera. One thing, however, that Bahati appreciated about all Kenyans was that despite their differences, they respected each other as people.

Bahati's family was among the middle class. Her father was a manager and her mother had an instructor's position at Natalie's Primary School, a local primary school. The headmaster was from Goa and had an open mind. He was a kind man, and not prejudiced toward others. Bahati's mother taught at Natalie's Primary School where Bahati and her brother, Mutuku, attended nursery first and then primary school. Prinina would arrive early in the morning to help get Bahati and her brother get ready for school. Later, when Mwikali was born, Prinina would take care of her while Bahati's mother and father worked during the day.

Bahati sat in the back and her brother in the front passenger seat of her mother's blue car. Every school morning, they traveled down Lang'ata Road past the two petrol stations and the road that turned off to Hardy Grocery store where Bahati's mother could purchase the Western cooking items that reminded her of America where she had grown up. Bahati's mother was good at finding bargains, and the family loved her cooking. Bahati recalled that, once they passed the old English house on the hill to the left of Natatlie's Primary School, they turned right onto a small road that led to the school. Bahati and Mutuku would jump out of the car, and go to the nursery school on campus, while her mother went to teach at the primary school. Bahati remembered taking naps during nursery school. She loved the afternoon snack and enjoyed her time in nursery. Later, when she went to Standard 1, 2, and 3, she was less amenable to school. Bahati could not read well like her older brother. Standard 1 was very hard for her and she was often embarrassed in class. Her favorite time was recess, when she would get to play with her friend Willie.

Bahati had a friend named Willie who was Kikuyu. They enjoyed playing together and would go to the back of schoolyard and buy sukari guru for one shilling, which Bahati saved from her pocket money. Later, as an adolescent, she was grateful for the times when she got pocket money. Once her father left his managerial job to campaign for office they did not get pocket money anymore. Bahati was thrilled to have a friend at school. Everything was fine until one day Bahati recalled hearing some boys say to Willie, "Hey Willie! Why are you hanging out with a girl?" Willie looked at Bahati and took his arm off of her and walked away. They usually walked around school with their arms across each other's shoulders. Bahati's face and heart fell, when Willie took his arm off of her. Willie realized that Bahati was a girl and that he would lose popularity with the first grade boys, if he continued to play with Bahati. Bahati felt a sharp prick of pain in her heart, because she had lost her only friend at school. Bahati was lost without Willie and would wander around school alone. She did not like to get up in the morning to attend classes. School was a chore!

Bahati continued to struggle with school and disliked reading a lot because it was hard for her. "Thhe-The, boouy-boy said jump," she would read as she attempted to sound out the words. As a result, Bahati was often frustrated and would talk to her classmates instead of listening to her teacher. She was very mischievous between Standard 1 and 3. She wanted to be liked by others and smart like her brother. It got so bad that one day Bahati told her father, "I do not want to go to school anymore. Instead I want to stay home and clean the house." Her father, who spoiled Bahati in her youth, agreed to her proposition, so for a few days Bahati stayed home and cleaned. She was happy because she was successful at something. Later, her mother insisted that she return to school, but she took Bahati's struggles to heart and went looking for a better school for Bahati. One afternoon after school, Bahati's mother told her she had visited her father's cousin at a school in Westlands. Mrs. Musomba, her father's cousin, was the secretary and helped to set up an appointment with the principal, Sister Jane. Bahati would have to be on her best behavior for this interview, but she was very excited to do so. Weeks after the interview, Bahati found out that she was going to school at Msongari. She was so excited, but little did she know it was the beginning of many good-byes and later some very sad days. Back at Moi Estate, Bahati rushed to tell Wanjiko of her new school. Wanjiko seemed calm and listened. They played together that day and had tea with Prinina and Florence like nothing ever happened. It was the beginning of their separation. Once Bahati moved from Moi Estate, a few years later, she never saw Wanjiko again; however, she thought of her often.

Bahati and her family continued to live in Moi Estate for two more years after she attended Msongari in Standard 3, and before they moved to their home in Lang'ata off of Magadi Road. Bahati enjoyed the evening sunsets at Moi Estate. The sun always set each night around seven p.m.. Before nightfall though, she and her friends would play in the road or at her friend's house. Bahati's mother would sometimes send Mutuku and her to the store around six p.m., which was about a mile away. Bahati would make sure they returned to the house before nightfall. Mwikali, Bahati's younger sister, would cry out, "Take me, I want to go too." Mutuku would tell her no, because she would beg for sweets at the store. Bahati's mother would cave in and send all three of them to keep Mwikali from screaming more. Bahati enjoyed walking down the first stretch of road, but always felt uncomfortable when they got to the corner by the stores. She had a sense in her heart and stomach that they were too far from home should danger find them. So whenever Bahati was at the store with her siblings, she would help them stay focused on getting what they needed so they could go home.

At the corner there were a few convenience stores, two butcheries, and a small clothing store with a hairdressing salon upstairs where Bahati got her hair braided with Raffia. Bahati's heart would jump when she went into the convenience store by the corner of the shopping area. She liked this store because it was well stocked. A kind hearted East Indian family owned it. Mutuku and Bahati would buy simple items like maize meal, sugar, milk, flour, and sweets for Mwikali when she cried out, "I want sweets." The butcher shop on the far end of the little shopping area was cleaner, but their meat did not seem as fresh as the other butchery. Bahati's mother always told them to get fresh meat, nothing bad. The butcher would cut off some goat meat or steak, depending on what Bahati's dad wanted to eat, and wrap it in white paper and send them off once they paid for the meat. The walk back was always quick and light. They had accomplished what they came for, and now they were walking home. The closer Bahati got to their little white house with the green roof, the lighter she felt in her step and heart. Mutuku was always brave, leading the way even when he did not want to. Bahati's father was very hard on him and did not always see through Mutuku's tender heartedness. Bahati and Mutuku were close in age and many people mistook them for twins.

On Saturdays Bahati would sometimes go to the hairdressing salon to get her hair braided. Her hair was short and did not grow unless it was in braids. Bahati remembered the feelings of inadequacy she sometimes experienced, whenever she went to the hairdressing salon. It was clear that she was half Kenyan and half African American, when she would speak. Her accent gave her away. She did not want to be mixed, but no matter how much she wanted to escape this, it was who she was. The girls and women would speak Kikuyu, Luo, or Kikamba, their tribal languages, with each other. Although the women were kind, Bahati felt embarrassed because she did not understand what they were saying nor could she speak any of their languages. She wanted to break out into a language other than Swahili or English, to let everyone know she was one of them. But she only knew Swahili and English, and this gave her away. She was different. In some ways, being from two cultures brought its challenges, and Bahati began to despise herself, because she so desperately wanted to fit in. "I wish I spoke Kikamba like Daddy, then I could talk to the other Kamba girls," Bahati would think to herself. Bahati was still young so these feelings of inadequacy would dissipate as fast as they emerged, and she would soon find herself admiring her hair. As she walked home she thought about how much her mother had to endure in order to fit into a new and foreign culture as she was from America. She admired her mother's ambition to learn Swahili quickly and learn the Akamba culture. She was a noble woman.

Bahati's mother worked hard to make their little house on the corner street of Moi Estate into a beautiful home. She even planted a garden of vegetables in the backyard. Bahati and her siblings played on the swing that their parents had brought back from America. Her father had studied at a university in America, where he met Bahati's mom. They married and returned to build Kenya, her father's dream. There were two leather seats on the swing, and one seesaw-like apparatus, which had two seats for each person to sit on when they swung. "I can swing up high," Mutuku would say. Bahati was afraid of heights but wanted to show that she could pump her legs and swing up high too. She would hold her breath, pump her legs, and swing up into the air. "I can go higher," Mutuku would say to her. But Bahati, knowing her limitations, would not take the bait. Mutuku, Mwikali, and Bahati enjoyed playing in the mud too. They made mud cakes and cooked them in the sun. "Kids come in," their mother would call as the sun set. Mutuku, Bahati, and Mwikali would come in for a hot meal that Bahati's mom had cooked.

After dinner they played with their mother, and then she read them a story. Bahati, however, would get hungry late at night, after they had all gone to bed. To get her mother's attention she would sing, "Mommy, where are you? I want some milk..." Bahati would sing the song until her mother came. Bahati enjoyed this time because it was just she and her mother, even though her mother was half asleep. Bahati would get her milk and some raisins and then go back to sleep. Sometimes, Bahati's mother would go to sleep before her father got home. Bahati's father would sometimes come home late at night, and she could tell that this saddened her mother. Bahati longed for her mother to know that she was there on her side to protect her from the pain she felt. She was happy though that despite their differences, her parents worked hard to keep the family together and eventually rose to help many people in their immediate family and community.

Bahati remembered many cousins, aunties, and uncles who lived with her family while she grew up. Bahati's young uncle who was training to become a medical doctor lived with her family in Lang'ata years later. He taught Mutuku and Bahati karate. Later, as an adult, Bahati appreciated that this was one of her first introductions to the Asian culture. Mumbua came to live also with Bahati's family when Bahati was seven-years-old. Mumbua was Bahati's cousin. Mumbua's mother and father were very kind people, but they could not afford to educate their daughter, so Bahati's father and mother offered to do this. Mumbua had a pleasant personality and brilliant smile.

She loved Bahati's mother and younger sister. Bahati struggled with jealousy as she felt her mother's attention was now split between Mwikali, Mutuku, Mumbua, and her. Bahati, however, kept these thoughts to herself as a child. Later, as an adolescent, Bahati had to revisit these feelings in order to begin to overcome her feelings of isolation and inadequacy. Overcoming those memories taught her to love again, especially those she cared about so much.

Bahati recollected the times that her parents would go out to the cocktail parties put on by her father's work. Bahati's mother would get all dressed up in her finest clothes and jewelry. Bahati's father had bought her mother ruby, gold, and ivory jewelry, which she wore to such events. When Bahati became an adult woman, her mother gave Bahati her 14-karat gold earrings and other fine pieces of jewelry. It took years for Bahati to wear the jewelry with confidence because she had felt so unattractive growing up. As a result, Bahati dressed very simply and plainly as an adolescent. But as an adult woman, married to a tenderhearted man who appreciated her inner and outer beauty, she felt she could wear the 14-karat gold earrings with confidence.

On party nights, Bahati would come in and play with her mother's makeup and jewelry and pretend to get ready to go out too. "Mom, you look pretty in your dress," Bahati would say. She loved watching her mother get ready to go out with her father. Bahati was happy to see her parents enjoy each other's company. Her father seemed excited, though also worried about good impressions. "Hurry up, honey, we need to get ready to go," her father would say. Bahati could only imagine the pressure her mother felt to be the perfect wife. Sometimes, Bahati could feel her stomach churn with emotional butterflies as she thought about the pressure her mother felt. But the shoes, dresses, suits, jewelry, and smiles all seemed to make the fears dissipate and the joy of seeing her parents work together to advance Bahati's father's career was enough for that brief moment. Soon the door was closed and they were off, and Mwikali, Mutuku, Mumbua, and Bahati would have to be in bed.

Mumbua called Bahati, Mwikali, and Mutuku, "You guys need to go to sleep now." Mwikali cried, "I don't want to!" Mumbua would comfort her. Mwikali loved having her back patted until she fell asleep, so Mumbua would do this to help Mwikali fall asleep. Bahati and Mutuku had bunk beds. Mutuku slept on the top and Bahati on the bottom. On occasion they would switch. The bunk bed had a ladder attached to it and Mutuku would climb up every night to get into the bed. There was a little railing along the side, but it was rather low. One day Bahati slept on the top bunk, and rolled over and fell out of bed. "Ouch!" Bahati recalled saying as she rubbed her head that night. She was startled, but climbed the ladder and went back to sleep.

Bahati and her family lived in Moi Estate for several years. They enjoyed many holidays together including Jamhuri Day and Christmas. Bahati's grandparents from Ukambani would come to visit often. Bahati's grandmother came to visit from America a couple of times. Once, Bahati's father and mother arranged a wonderful safari for her grandmother from America. She got to visit Tsavo, see the wild animals, and stay in a beautiful hotel. Grandma Berry, as they called her, was very happy to see her family. Over the years, Grandma Berry would write to the family, send packages, or call. Whenever Bahati's mom would get the package slip in the mailbox, they would drive down to the package area and pick up Grandma's gift. She would often send American candy, which they enjoyed as a family. Bahati remembers hearing the phone ring and her mother saying, "Grandma's on the phone." The children would all run up to the rotary phone and take turns talking to her. Once while Grandma Berry visited, Bahati's family showed her the new family home in Lang'ata, which they were building. Bahati remembers walking on the foundation of the house with her grandmother, and how years later it was amazing to see that something so sturdy that withstood the earthquake in Nairobi in the early 80s came from a simple foundation.

Moi Estate was in many ways Bahati's foundation for how to live among people of different races, tribes, social economic statuses, and ages. From the little corner store at the end of the street, to playing in Wanjiko's home, and eating Prinina's Ugandan matoke and fish, Bahati learned that all kinds of people could live together. In Moi Estate Bahati learned the simple pleasures of being a neighbor, nothing fancy, nothing to show off, just enjoyment and laughter. She learned that while life brings moments like those in the braid shop when her obvious differences made her feel left out, it also brought moments that made her feel connected through the Prininas and the Wanjikos of the world, people who saw her as a person, a friend, someone to laugh and enjoy life with. Life also brought her the East Indian storeowners and her neighbors across the street that shared their family's culture and generosity. Yes, Moi Estate was a special time for Bahati and her family. Many simple memories, from Grandma Berry visiting from America, to Umau and Susu coming up from Kibwezi to celebrate Christmas, to walking down to the corner store, to playing with friends from different tribes and races. Bahati thought to herself, "There are not many towns like Moi Estate." It was a neighborhood to remember, it was Moi Estate!

VIGNETTE NUMBER TWO
A Holiday to Remember

Holidays! "The word sounds like ice cream melting down my hand on a hot summer day," Bahati thought to herself. They're called vacations or holidays depending on where you live, but in Nairobi they are called holidays. Bahati was just ten years old then and the Christmas holidays were about to come. Miriam had celebrated Eid just a few months earlier and had invited Bahati and her friends over to the house. In Nairobi in the early 70s and 80s, everyone lived together and somehow got along despite their racial, tribal, and religious differences. Aimée, Agnes, Njeri, Kina, and Miriam were all friends of Bahati and were excited about the holidays coming up in December. Aimée was the youngest in the class of fifth graders. Just as her name meant, "loved" in French, their small group of friends looked out for Aimée when her father died and cherished her as a younger sister. After the funeral, her mother returned to Europe, but later returned to Kenya to raise Aimée. Kenya had become home, and Aimée's mother felt safer raising her daughter in the foreign land she had become so familiar with. Like many expatriates, Kenya became a home for them in the 80s.

Agnes's family was from a small island off the coast of Kenya. Her family had moved to Kenya during the time of independence. Agnes came from a humble family and was a solid friend to Bahati during her time at school. Agnes treasured things deep in her soul but did not always share them, but Bahati could read them on her face. Agnes was blonde with blue eyes, but because her family was not from Europe, she did not always get the free hand given to wealthy children of European decent. Bahati could tell this frustrated Agnes a lot. But Bahati, being brown skinned with brown eyes, felt confused because if Agnes could not accept herself for who she was—and she was beautiful—then where was Bahati in all this? Sometimes Bahati wanted Agnes to be happy with herself just so that Bahati could feel the same. These were the silent struggles of a fifth grader about to become an adolescent, searching for an identity of her own. Bahati could slough off comments like the one Jane made one day, "you have thick lips Bahati," and then burst out laughing. Jane had thin, almost nonexistent lips. Later in life, Bahati would find it curious that some women had lip surgery to widen their thin lip lines. Now in her apartment room far from Ngong Hills, Bahati thought to herself, "People, we are never happy with ourselves, yet we have to make others feel our misery." Bahati paused and then brought her thoughts back to Agnes. Agnes was like Bahati in many ways. She wanted to be accepted by her people, her race. Bahati wanted to be fully Akamba or fully African American, she did not want to be mixed. She wanted her people to appreciate her for who she was that her brown skin was brown enough, her curly hair was curly enough, and her stubby ski-jump nose was stubby enough. But like Agnes, she would have to find that inner peace with Mulungu's help. It was Agnes who once told Bahati, after a game of tennis together on the school tennis courts, "Bahati, you have to know that you are loved by God. You can't please people; you need to excel for you. Don't worry what people think." Bahati remembered those lines, and between the encouragement from Agnes and Bahati's other friends, Bahati began to excel in school for the first time in her life. She thought, "I am not the smartest, the prettiest, or the brightest, but I can try my hardest." And she did.

"Aimée what are you doing for the holidays?" Miriam asked. "We are going to Mombasa."

Bahati thought to herself, *Wow! That sounds wonderful, I wish my family were going to the coast too.* "Agnes what are you doing?" Bahati asked.

"Spending time with my family."

Bahati knew Agnes was sincere as Agnes's family loved each other and were close.

"Bahati, what are you doing?" asked Kina.

"Well, I know we are going to celebrate Christmas. Mom already bought the Christmas tree and set out the advent calendar, so we are counting down the days, but the rest is a mystery."

Kina was Hindu and did not celebrate Christmas but was going to enjoy the time with her family in Naivasha, where they had a home. Njeri was going to go up country to visit her grandmother in Nyeri, and Miriam was traveling to Canada to see her relatives. "I'll miss you all, but I am looking forward to not getting up at six a.m. to get ready for school," Bahati said.

Aimée shouted out, "I am looking forward to not doing homework," and the group said in unison, "That's right!" Aimée's mom pulled up at three p.m. to pick her up. Agnes walked home because she lived nearby. Kina's and Miriam's drivers pulled up to take them home, Njeri went home with her older sister, and Bahati's dad, Amani, pulled up in his white Peugeot. The holidays were officially on!

Bahati sat in the backseat where she always sat. She looked out the window at the bougainvillea that lined the driveway up to the school and main road. Her father made a left turn and they headed home. They passed Lavington Shopping Center, where her father and mother would sometimes stop off after school to get treats for the ride home. Bahati was thrilled to be on her holidays. She did not know what they would bring. She wished she could be in Mombasa or travel to the Maasai Mara as she had done once before, but she knew that was not happening this holiday. She did feel enthused despite the fact that her family had not planned an extravagant holiday trip. They would spend the holiday as a family, the way they usually did. As it was not the planting season, Bahati and her siblings did not have to work in the garden or on the farm. They could relax, and this thrilled Bahati. She disliked pulling weeds during the planting season. "Ouch," Bahati thought to herself as she remembered pricking her fingers on the thorns from the weeds that she pulled up. When Bahati left home, years later, she did not garden much but she would reflect on internal weeds that pricked her heart; weeds of greed, jealousy, and fear. Bahati worked diligently to pull these weeds from her heart so that she could build strong relationships with others.

Bahati brought her thoughts back to her holiday to remember. It was just about four p.m. when Bahati's father pulled into the driveway and parked the car. It was teatime, an old English tradition that many Kenyans still practiced. Mom was in a good mood. She had made some gingerbread boys, thin-sliced butter and jam sandwiches, and some hot chai tea. Along with the glorious gift of delicious food, Mama Ana was stopping by with her children. Mama Ana was close friends with Bahati's mother, Mary, and lived near Natalie's Primary School, where Mary taught and her children went to school. Mama Ana and Mary, Bahati's mother, were both African American women married to Bantu—Kenyan men—and could emphathize with each other's feelings. They shared the same history. The United States of America, where they came from, was changing so much in the 1970s; African American women and men were gaining more freedom. In Kenya, the people had just received their independence in 1963 and were still trying to find out who they were in the random boundary lines that had been drawn for tribes to live in. Hence; there was tension sometimes among the tribes. Bahati's mom and Mama Ana worked this out together and worked to be respectful of others while maintaining what they thought was best for women in the community, especially themselves.

Bahati whispered, "Tea's ready. Would anyone like some gingerbread boys, fruitcake, or thin-sliced butter and jam sandwiches?"

"Mmm! That sounds yummy," everyone said, and then they sat down to eat.

"What are you doing for the holidays, Mary?" Mama Ana asked.

"Oh just staying in town and with family. Amani's family is coming up from Kibwezie and Machakos. We are looking forward to a full house, and my mom will be visiting from the States. It'll be nice to see her again and see her with everyone."

"Sounds like a beautiful time."

Mama Ana spoke, "Bahati, by the way, here is the 70 shillings I owe you for the eggs. I hope you can buy something nice for your parents."

"Thanks, Mama Ana, I will." Bahati thought it was generous of Mama Ana to pay Bahati even though she and her family were going through hard times financially. Bahati, however, could not find it in herself to let go of the money because she wanted to buy something nice for her mother and father for the holidays. Bahati had worked hard on her little business selling chicken eggs so she could buy presents for those she loved. Later, as Bahati grew, she realized what it cost Mama Ana so that Bahati could be generous toward her family. She would read a parable many years later about a widow who gave her last pennies and how, in comparison to the rich who gave a small portion of their wealth, this widow was held in high esteem by Love, Compassion, and Human-Kindness. Bahati longed to imitate Mama Ana's heart, as she grew older and wiser with time and age.

A few days later, Bahati looked out the kitchen window and she could see Umau and Susu, her father's parents, walking down the driveway. They walked hand in hand. Umau leaned on his walking stick as they strolled down the driveway together. They had come a long way from Ukambani to Lang'ata in Nairobi. They had walked from Mukoma Road where the local bus, the matatu, had dropped them off. Prior to that, they had walked from the dirt road in Kibwezi to the Mombasa Highway where they could catch a matatu to Nairobi. It was generally better to take the Kenya Bus, but matatus were in business and offered a cheaper fair, so Susu and Umau took the matatu. Bahati jumped to see Susu and Umau.

Susu always calmed Bahati's soul, as she was a quiet and gentle woman. She never argued with anyone or became frustrated, but was always patient and kind. Umau had lots of energy, even for an older man. He was also full of opinions as he was the elder in the family. So Wisdom and Humility strolled down the driveway hand-in-hand telling their own generational stories from their personal and married lives. "Waa Cha," Susu and Umau said to everyone and the children answered, "Aaa." Formal greetings were common in Kenyan tribal cultures, and Bahati's Kamba culture insisted that the elders greet the children with this special greeting. Bahati led her grandparents down the living room, stairs and into the living room, where they sat and had tea with milk and sugar. Susu proceeded to tell Bahati and her siblings an Akamba story about a man who helped the needy. She told them that the story reminded her of their father because he had helped his siblings and many other people, and that Life had blessed him with a noble wife and lovely home.

Mary, Bahati's mother, came home with ingredients for several holiday dishes. It was the Christmas holidays in Nairobi and Bahati's family celebrated Christmas. They had put up the Christmas tree a few weeks earlier. When Bahati moved to the northern hemisphere, she learned that Christmas trees in Kenya look very different from the Christmas trees in the northern hemisphere. The branches are not as full as trees found in the northern hemisphere because Kenya lies close to the equator and it is very hot. Most plants have evolved so that they can store water for long periods of time, and the Christmas trees in Kenya are typical of plants living in that area. Bahati's family decorated the tree with stringed popcorn that they had popped in the pot with a little olive oil. The other Christmas ornaments were hanging on the tree alongside the ones they had made by hand as a family. On top of the tree was the morning star for hope.

Mary put the ingredients away, and then came and sat down with Umau and Susu. She had Bahati put on the record of *Ave Maria* by Maria Callas, which they listened to on the record player they had brought back from America, while they talked as a family. Bahati thought to herself, "This is a peaceful moment. I will always remember it," and she did. Mary could not speak Kikamba, the language spoken by the Akamba, Susu, Umau, and her father, so she spoke to them in Swahili. Umau knew Swahili, but Susu knew only a little. They talked for a while about their trip from Ukambani to Nairobi. Then Mary and Bahati went into the kitchen to join Bahati's aunties and help prepare dinner.

It was just a few days before Christmas, and Mary's mother had flown in from her hometown in America. Bahati was thrilled to have her Grandma Berry, Susu, and Umau with her and the family. Grandma Berry had pressed hair that looked very fine. Grandma Berry wore a smart knee-length dress and always wore her shoes in the house. Susu was different. She wore a simple dress with a Kamba designed sheet cloth, a shuka, garbed around her neck and across the back of her dress. Both women were beautiful and unique in their own way. Umau always wore the same black suit that Bahati's father had bought him. Umau wore it with pride. Together with Mary and Amani, Bahati's father, the six of them all sat together for a while and discussed family affairs. Amani was the only one who spoke all three languages: English, Swahili, and Kikamba. He spoke other Kenyan tribal languages, too, as he was a very smart man. Bahati stared into the eyes of her grandparents and she could see their inner pride for her parents, their son and daughter. Bahati was glad that they had all come and that the family was together. It was going to be a holiday to remember!

Christmas Eve came and Bahati's family sang Christmas hymns, carols, and prayed at the midnight service. The midnight service was always her favorite. Everyone in town would come all dressed up and ready to be together for the holidays. Bahati especially enjoyed getting dressed up and singing the holiday songs. She enjoyed listening to the lead vocalist direct the congregation in song. She had a beautiful soprano voice. She was from Goa and had olive skin with shoulder-length dark hair. After the service, Bahati and her family all piled into the family car and pickup truck. The whole family had come, so they had other relatives to transport who were visiting from out of town. Amani insisted that everyone in the family attend the midnight service, and so they did.

Once they were home, Bahati and her siblings were rushed to bed. In Bahati's family, unlike her Kamba cousins, they believed in Santa Claus. This was a reflection of Bahati's mother's American culture. Her parents told the children that they had to go to bed if they wanted Santa Claus to come. Mary had been shopping all month long, looking for bargains and special items that would encourage everyone when the whole Amani family and clan would awake in the morning to gifts. Once the children went to bed, Mary proceeded to the kitchen to cook the turkey, another American tradition. In Bahati's home they had Kamba and American traditions, and the family meals reflected both cultures. The next day, Bahati's brother and the other men in the family butchered a goat; it was a Kamba tradition to have goat at every celebration. Bahati's aunties cooked chapattis, mboga, and tripe stew. Mary spent the day before making more gingerbread, cakes, cookies, sweet potato pie, mashed potatoes, gravy, and lots of salad with ingredients grown on the family farm. It was going to be a feast.

The next morning, Mutuku was the first one down the stairs, and then came Bahati and Mwikali. They found their treasures hidden under the tree. Santa Claus had come and Mary had made sure everyone had something to open. Bahati had not forgotten her parents. She bought her father a fancy pen and her mother a lovely book, as her mother loved to read. Bahati was happy that she could contribute to the giving and generosity. She was happy to see her mother receive a gift, though she seemed distracted by all the day's work. Bahati hoped she would notice the book when things settled down and were less hectic. After they opened their gifts, Mutuku got on the phone to call their cousins who also lived nearby. They talked for a long time about what they were each going to do for the day. Muoma and his family were going to slay a goat, too, and he was looking forward to helping with this task, as he was now old enough. Bahati went into the kitchen to see what needed to be done, and Mwikali played in the living room with Susu and Grandma Berry. The sun was shinning, the turkey had put out a warm aroma in the kitchen, and everyone was in a good mood. It was going to be a pleasant day.

The day went on and soon the goat meat was roasting on the fire. Bahati was asked to make the kashumba to go along with the goat meat. Kashumba is a pleasant and spicy dipping sauce that goes with goat meat and other meats. Amani sat on the veranda talking with his father and mother-in-law. Susu liked to be indoors and stayed with the children. Bahati wanted her mother to rest, so she encouraged her to relax and have a seat with daddy. Her mother finally did. The children played outside for a while, and the grown-ups all migrated to the veranda. Everyone was talking and laughing. Bahati could hear Grandma Berry, Father, Umau, Susu, Mother, and her aunties and uncles all talking and laughing. She could see her brother and sisters playing joyfully. Bahati's youngest sister had just been born and played in the crib. Bahati thought to herself, "This is a lovely day." She could see the Ngong Hills in the distance and the sun was about to set. It was about six p.m. in the evening and night would fall within the hour. Bahati closed her eyes and promised to never forget that day and to share it with others. It was a beautiful day, a day full of wonderful memories, including all things Kamba: respecting your elders, enjoying a lovely meal as a family, and singing songs to Mulungu.

The next few days were spent cleaning up the house from the big festivities. Before Grandma Berry went home, Bahati's father took her and the rest of the family to see the Kamba dancers just outside of Machakos. The Kamba dancers are known throughout Kenya and the world for their acrobatic maneuvers and magnificent drumbeats. Bahati enjoyed the performance that day. After the performance there was a Kamba pop group that sang and played. It was nice to hear and Bahati and her sibling swayed on the dance floor. They soon left and headed down toward Kibwezi to drop off Umau and Susu. They stayed the night in Kibwezi. Amani had built a stone house with a tin roof for his parents, but they also lived in their Kamba huts that were made of mud and sticks. The roofs were made of long pieces of Savannah grass. Bahati remembers sleeping on the cot on the dirt floor, which felt very different from her warm bed and tile floor in her home in Lang'ata. This was an amazing life; Bahati could experience both the past and the present of the Kamba people in Kenya. The next morning they got in the car and drove back to Nairobi. On the way they saw zebra and impala grazing in the distance, along the Mombasa Highway. Once they were back in Nairobi, Grandma Berry packed her bags and was soon boarding her flight back to America. It had been a wonderful visit for her and the family. Bahati was grateful that she had had the chance to see her Grandma Berry again. It would be several years before she would see her again in person.

The holidays were soon over, and the Christmas tree was put into the composting hole to be recycled into the soil. The ornaments were returned to the Christmas box and put away for the following year. Bahati was sad that the holidays were over, but she was glad that her Grandma Berry had come to see her and the family. She was grateful to see her Susu and Umau as well, along with her aunties and cousins. Soon she was looking forward to going back to school in a few weeks. She would see her friends again and hear about their holidays and travels. Bahati would tell them how she had enjoyed the company of her family, with a special guest appearance from Grandma Berry. This was definitely a holiday for Bahati and her family to remember for years to come!

School resumed and Bahati drove up the school driveway lined by pink bougainvillea. Her heart beat steady and it seemed like butterflies were fluttering in her stomach as the car drove up to the main campus building. The first day of school was always exciting and everyone shared their holiday stories with each other. Bahati looked forward to sharing about her time with her family, her trip to Kibwezi, and dancing to Kamba pop songs on the dance floor outside of Machakos. She was also eager to hear about her friends' trips to Mombasa, Naivasha, Nyeri, and Canada. Bahati was eager to share the sweets that her Grandma Berry had brought from America for the holidays. The sweets from America were unique with flavor and different from the sweets that they ate in Nairobi. Bahati was sure that her friends would be thrilled. As the car drove up to the school building, Bahati stepped out and ran to her waiting friends.

VIGNETTE NUMBER THREE
Gordon's Captain

Bahati struggled with competiveness. As a young child and adolescent, she was never happy with herself because she felt others did not like her for who she was. "Janet is prettier and smarter than me. Maybe if I straighten my hair, win the swim race, or play a good game of netball Janet and the other girls will notice me," Bahati would often find herself thinking. She put a lot of effort into being accepted. It took many life lessons to teach Bahati that she did not have to be accepted by everyone in order to live in peace with herself.

Bahati first began to learn this lesson when she was in Standard 7, the grade when she could finally run for team captain. There were four teams in the school, and she was a member of the blue team. The blue team was called Gordon. Bahati was not the most popular girl at school, but she had some friends among her peers and the younger girls. Her school was an all-girls school, which built confidence in the students to become strong women in the future. Unfortunately, it also brought more opportunities for the cattiness that girls struggle with at times. Bahati was sometimes an instigator of catty behavior, but often she was the recipient. Judith was a bully in the school and often went after Bahati. "Hi, Bahati. Your blouse is not tucked in, it's hanging out of your skirt. Oh! By the way your shoes are untied, too. You don't look like a Msongari girl today. I don't think you can ever be team captain of anything," Judith said one day at school. The girls standing with Judith burst out laughing. Bahati listened to their laughter and saw their white teeth shining in their mouths as they laughed. Bahati felt humiliated inside and attempted to fix herself up so she could be a Msongari girl. Luckily, Bahati benefited from the favor of more socially adept friends like Njeri and Agnes. Njeri would often come to Bahati's rescue. On that particular day, Bahati recalled Njeri retorting back to Judith, "A Msongari girl is a kind person, who speaks with uplifting words. Obviously your words to Bahati were not kind. Perhaps it is you who should evaluate if you are a Msongari Girl." Bahati smiled brightly at Njeri, while Judith and her friends walked off in embarrassment. It was friends like Agnes and Njeri who helped Bahati believe she could run for team captain that year, and so she did. After a younger school vote, Bahati was made the team captain of Gordon. It was the only year that Bahati was the captain or leader of anything at school during her entire primary and secondary education. This is the story of how Bahati became team captain and the life lessons that she learned while she was captain.

The bell rang at eight a.m. and Bahati and the rest of the school all lined up in the assembly hall for the morning gathering. Bahati lined up with the other girls in Standard 7. This was the highest class in primary school before she would graduate and attend secondary school. The assembly hall was a large room with several doors at the back for the students to file through after assemblies in the morning. The light would shine brilliantly through the windows on the doors and up high on the walls closest to the ceiling. It felt like one big family as the girls stood in rows from kindergarten through Standard 7 and talked with each other while they waited for assembly to start. They sang their morning song, said morning prayers, listened to the head mistress instruct them on the day, and then filed out to class. Bahati would always find herself day-dreaming before assembly started. Bahati loved to think a lot. She often daydreamed of complex and challenging issues in society. Her family enjoyed reading several international newspapers and magazines. One particular morning, Bahati found herself thinking about the turbulent times that year around the world with many countries in conflict with each other. She pondered on how little the world seemed to have learned from World War II and was afraid of a nuclear war between the countries that considered themselves super powers. Bahati felt powerless in the world, and perhaps this is what drove her partly to want to be a team captain. In her own way, she would have some opportunity to help create a safer and better world. Bahati thought she would do this through leadership. She did not yet know the importance and beauty of altruism. Her competitive spirit and feelings of inferiority often left her thinking she needed to be a leader to be effective. In time, though, life taught her to have compassion toward people in order to be truly effective. She learned that she just had to think of others long enough to care and help them in their time of need.

"People need to be loved and cared for so they feel safe," Bahati thought to herself as she stared up at the ceiling. "Bahati, it's time to sing," Anges said as she tapped Bahati on the shoulder and brought her out of her daydream. Bahati said thank you and began singing with the other girls. One of Bahati's favorite songs was sung that morning, "All Things Bright and Beautiful." It was a pleasant hymn about how God had created things beautiful and bright in all sizes, shapes, textures, and bounty. After the song, the head mistress prayed and made the day's announcements. She reminded the students in Standard 7 that the exam on the Certificate of Primary Education (CPE) was coming up at the end of the year. It was a known fact that many students who performed poorly and came from low-income families were very likely not going to get a coveted spot in secondary school. This was very depressing for the girls. So, though seventh grade was the grade that the girls got to be leaders, it was a sober year as they knew they had to pass the CPE to continue in their education. The headmistress went on to let the girls know that they would be picking school-wide team captains for the various sports activities, including the swimming gala and track and field sports day.

As it was the early part of the year, the swimming gala was coming up and the teams would race each other for the school trophy.

When assembly ended, Bahati and the girls were excited about the swimming gala and elections.

"Agnes, do you think Gordon can win this year?" Bahati asked as they walked to class.

Aimée chimed in, "Not so fast, Bahati. The yellow team is going to win this year."

"We'll see about that!" Bahati said.

"Quiet!" The school prefect said to the three of them as they chattered while they walked single file back to class. Bahati silenced herself and her thoughts went back to the other topics covered in the assembly that morning. She was not too shaken by the CPE as she believed it would be abolished by the time she took the test. This, of course, was wishful thinking, which many adolescents struggle with when they don't want to deal with something difficult. Bahati's siblings were much smarter than she was and Bahati felt intellectually inferior to them. She pretended that she did not care about her education because it seemed that everyone expected her to do about average. And as a result, she did. She was, however, excited about the thought of being team captain. One thing that excited her was the opportunity to be popular and accepted by the crowd, and the other was to try to be a good leader and do something positive. Bahati hoped to build up her self-esteem through leadership. Little did Bahati know that it takes a leader with a pure heart to lead people, who are often complicated and have all kinds of agendas and motives for why they want you to be their leader. Yes, being team captain was the beginning of Bahati understanding her own heart for leadership, the blessings of being second, and the inner peace that comes from serving people rather than telling people what to do.

The Standard 7 girls had a long walk to their classroom from the assembly hall. Bahati's classroom was on the secondary side of campus, about a half-mile away from the primary school campus. Once they got to the secondary side of campus, Bahati and her classmates walked up a beautiful flight of stairs to get to their classroom on the second floor. Their class was right above Sister Beth's office. Sister Beth was the secondary school's headmistress. The girls were always on their best behavior as they climbed the stairs for fear of detention or any unnecessary consequences brought about from acting silly while walking to class. Aimée and Bahati forgot and started to chatter again as they walked back to class. "Ssh!" Agnes said. "We are getting close to Sister Beth's office and she will hear us making noise if we are not quiet. We don't want detention, so zip it, Aimée and Bahati."

Once Bahati and her classmates passed Sister Beth's office and were in their class, they settled into the day. They said good morning to Mrs. Narona, their classroom teacher, curtseyed to her, and sat down in their seats. Mrs. Narona had the girls nominate potential candidates among their peers for team captains. There were four teams that needed captains. Bahati had longed and tried to be a vice captain, when she was in Standard 6, but did not succeed. This year she was a little more hopeful and, sure enough, her name was among those picked for the blue team Gordon. The names were submitted to the entire Gordon team: from Standard 7 down to kindergarten. Everyone had to vote and give their votes to their classroom leaders, who would count the votes with their teachers' help. A few days passed before Bahati heard the news. Donna came running up to Bahati and said, "The tallies are in. Bahati, you are team captain." Bahati was officially the captain of the Gordon team. She felt so confident and sure of herself at that moment. She usually slouched, but she stood up tall at the moment and thought to herself, "I'm team captain! Wow! They do like me!" Later, however, her inner struggles with insecurity and competiveness would rear their heads, and Bahati would learn to serve rather than boast about being a leader.

Bahati's vice captain was picked that day, as well as the rest of the Gordon leadership team. The first event they had to prepare for was the swimming gala. Gordon had won before, but not lately.

Aimée was on the yellow team and she was an excellent swimmer, as were other members of her team. Agnes was a member of the green team, and Njeri was a member of the red team. Bahati felt the pressure to lead Gordon to victory, but she herself was not the best swimmer. She was an average swimmer and had won only a few medals at swim meets. Bahati's fear led to competitiveness and doubt that Gordon could win against such strong competitors. She thought she would pull the team together and motivate them with competiveness.

"We're going to win, everyone. You need to practice during swim class. I want everyone to do 10 laps for practice. We need to win this for Gordon!" The Gordon team stared at her in disbelief when Bahati said 10 laps, especially the little girls in standard 1 and 2. Then her vice captain, Francesca, spoke up and encouraged Bahati to let everyone swim her best instead of worrying about the competitor on the other team. "Bahati, why don't we let the girls swim their best at the swimming gala. Not everyone can get 10 laps in, especially the younger students," Francesca said.

"*Yes, Bahati! What Francesca said makes sense,*" responded Gordon's leadership team.

Bahati felt pressured by the numbers and said, "Okay!" Francesca also encouraged Bahati to help the team pull together and have the best swimmer in each category elect to swim that race, instead of everyone competing against the other. Bahati's team started to grow stronger. Some girls realized it would be best for them to cheer and let a better swimmer swim the race than complain and fight over a place in the competition. In the end, Gordon won the swimming Gala. Bahati was thrilled, but she knew it was the vice captain's input that had actually led the team to victory, which made her jealous of Francesca, the vice captain. Bahati did not like this about herself; she didn't want to be jealous of others' success. "Oh! I hate that ugly feeling I get when someone does something better than me," Bahati said to herself. Bahati noticed that Francesca was becoming popular among the girls in the Gordon team, and there were rumors that they wanted her for their team captain. This made Bahati feel inferior, like she was not good enough. "I can't even lead a team to victory on my own," Bahati thought to herself. In a few months, after the swimming gala event, the Gordon team elected Francesca as team captain. Bahati was sad, but later she was glad for a chance to learn what it meant to lead. "Oh! I wish I had done a better job, but at least I had a chance," Bahati thought. She pondered about leadership. "It is a service, a chance to bring people together and help them reach their full potential." Bahati learned to appreciate, too, that people had seen the good she could do, for they had elected her as leader. She did not have to trust in the approval of others to feel at peace with herself. She had done her best. She had listened to her vice captain and put her advice into action instead of giving into her pride and insisting on her own way of doing things. As a result, Gordon had won. Bahati had learned the treasure of being humble and lifting others up above herself so that the team could be great! Bahati led and Gordon had won. In the end Bahati felt satisfied, for Gordon's victory was the goal and purpose of her leadership!

VIGNETTE NUMBER FOUR
A Walk by the River

The River to Freedom

The River, it never stops, and life is always available from it.
The River, which flows freely downhill into the sea.
The River carries my hope, will I let go and follow its path?

Long before I knew the River, I knew struggles inner and outer,
struggles with animosity and imperfection.
Animosity almost left me breathless,
and certainly incapable of loving.

Life showed me I needed grace and truth; I needed free love,
a Lamb's choice to set me free.

But to receive the results of grace and truth, I would have to
embrace honesty and innocence through Mulungu's way.

I cannot buy my way in, sell my way in, or cheat my way in.
I cannot attempt to simplify perfection
by pretending I have no faults.
And ignoring my imperfections left me
with painful sores and wounds.

I lived a hypocritical lie desiring to be immaculate,
but constant reminders from onus awoke
me to my nightmare of hypocrisy and imperfection.

But now tired and worn, a walk to the river seemed good. A walk toward grace and truth, A walk in Mulungu's paths. A walk down to the River of Life!

Bahati lived in Lang'ata during her middle and adolescent years. Like most adolescents, school and home life and hormonal, physical, and cognitive changes impacted Bahati's ability to build close relationships with others. This was compounded by her insecurities during her middle childhood. She did have a few friends who inspired her and kept her head above water while she was in adolescence. At her family home in Lang'ata, her room was her haven, but her walks to the river and through the neighborhood were her peace. She could see the Ngong Hills from her bedroom window and would watch the sun set and rise in the morning. Sometimes she would even see a zebra or two trotting across the luscious plain.

Bahati looking out the window

The images of the Ngong Hills, the river flowing at the bottom of the farm, and the beautiful tailored gardens along the neighborhood streets quieted the turbulence Bahati felt inside and around her. Unlike Moi Estate, each neighbor in Lang'ata had at least ten or more acres of land to live on, so neighbors were each tucked in their homes, usually large mansions, and often not seen. Bahati was lonely for friendship, but during this time she learned that Mulungu was a comfort in times of trouble, and in time she found inner peace.

"Come on Kidogo, Kwezi, Getta, and Karen, let's go for a walk by the river," Bahati would often say to her dogs. Kidogo was the shortest one with the curliest black hair who often jumped up and down indicating that he wanted to go outside. He was the only dog allowed in the family home, as he was too small to live outside. Kwezi, Getta, and Karen were Alsatians and stood strong with confidence. Once Bahati put on her shoes, she and the dogs would all head out toward the river for their walk. There were several paths to the river, but Bahati liked to take the walking trail that had been paved by people's trips to the river and the small town where her mother sent the gardener to buy groceries. To get to the river, Bahati would pass the chicken house, and cow house and then come to the fence that separated the house, farm, and farmhouses from the backwoods. All five of them would brave the tall grass, stones, and possible snakes as they walked to the river. The dogs could always tell when Bahati needed a walk to soothe her soul. They would bark and wag their tails to go running to the river. They were her friends and protectors.

Once they got to the river, they walked through the river and stepped on the stones that led to the small village on the other side of the river. The tree that stood by the river was luscious and had many wild branches. Bahati, however, was always scared of a snake popping out of the grass, as the vegetation down by the river had not been cut back. A baby python and its mother had once chased her on the sidewalk by the house and Bahati did not want to meet another one down by the river. But her walks to the river and around the neighborhood brought her greater peace than fear. Peace always seemed to win out, and she wanted that peace to keep going and settle her spirit, soul, and mind.

Bahati's struggle with anxiety caused much of her restlessness. Later in life, while she was in college, Bahati learned that life progresses with common and individual differences for the adolescent and young adult. Familiar relationships and interrelationships begin to change. People struggle with their own inabilities to regulate their emotions and perceive their temperament styles. In adolescence, many children don't have a voice to articulate these challenges, and they either externalize or internalize their behaviors. Bahati internalized hers. She was the type of person who kept everything inside. She compensated for her internal pain and anger by not arguing out loud with others. Often times Bahati would argue in her head while her foes taunted her. "You can't hurt me," Bahati would think. "Yes, I can," Bahati would imagine her foe retorting back. "No you can't!" Bahati would think to herself. This made for a very tumultuous adolescent and adult life for Bahati. It was easier to fight with people inside her mind, where she was more powerful. Outside, she was a victim to their rage and did not have the power to subdue them. As a young child, she acted out her frustrations by being mischievous with no care for what people thought of her. Sister Beth liked this about Bahati and often said Bahati was "genuine and real, not a pretender." As Bahati got older, she could see the pain that others endured. She thought taking the pain on herself was her way of coping, of giving the other person time to heal, time to come to her senses. Some people did; in other instances, Bahati is still waiting. It took Mulungu to teach Bahati how to hold true to grace and truth so she could have compassion for those hurting around her. She was not the sacrificial lamb she thought she had to be, but she did have to learn compassion. She did not have to endure everyone's anger and hatred, but she did have to learn how to regulate her own feelings about the events surrounding her.

Bahati once gave into her bitterness as an adolescent. She remembered an argument she had with Beatrice, a nemesis to Bahati during her adolescence. Beatrice was not afraid to be aggressive and did not fear the consequences of her actions on Bahati. One day it came to a head. "Bahati, where are you!" Beatrice shouted. Bahati groveled up to Beatrice, who was physically larger than her. Bahati thought to herself as she approached, and then felt a stinging sensation on her face where Beatrice had just slapped her. "My angry foe is at my soul's door again to strike me with hate, and I don't know what to do. My own anger is rushing through me, and today a new emotion has emerged: hate. It tastes so cold, nothing warm about this emotion. Anger always felt a little like fire or lightning going off in my soul, but now anger is pressing in on me and the cold animosity in me rises, banging at my heart's door for freedom into my soul, promising protection from the anger of others. I remember what I learned in religion class: love, love, and love. But I have tried, and what has love gotten me? Anger is still at my soul's door." Bahati burst out crying and ran to console herself with angry thoughts towards Beatrice. Little did Bahati know that each time she refused to forgive someone, she let go of love and allowed bitterness to creep into her heart and steal her joy. Now she was angry and bitter, like her foe.

Bahati decided to release the emotionless feeling of resentment and apathy into her heart that day, as she could not bear the pain anymore. "I will detach myself from the pain I feel and hide behind my empty feelings," she thought. "I can't bear this pain anymore." As she released the odious emotions she felt toward Beatrice, a hot burning sensation emerged in her heart and she could feel a cold sensation beginning to fill her soul, heart, spirit, and mind. Her heart felt hard like a rock. "What have I done?" Bahati thought to herself. "It's too late. I can't find moist feelings of forgiveness and love in my heart. The coldness from the hatred is too cold and hard to bear." She felt her chest tighten in that moment. It was hard to breathe for a moment, and in that moment a part of Bahati died. It would take several years before Bahati would trust again and feel the warmth of love in her heart.

During those years of coldness, fear, and anger, Bahati's closest friends were her pets and farm animals. She was responsible for taking care of the hens that laid eggs. The hens would fight to keep their eggs, even though they were not going to hatch. Bahati always thought it was curious how protective the hens were of their eggs. Her heart was so cold then that if anyone was fighting for her peace of mind, she was so lost she could not perceive it. She longed for it, though. Thinking back, Bahati remembered several walks that she and her dogs had taken through the Lang'ata neighborhood, past several homes in Lang'ata on a long paved road. One day, Bahati went walking because fear and jealousy had overcome her. Taunting was at her door and she could not fight back without turning to hate. Ever since she had turned to hate, she could not hold back other dark emotions, nor did she want to. They filled her heart, soul, and mind. Jealousy, bitterness, and self-pity were frequent visitors to her spirit. Her spirit was weakening and she could not say no to these emotions. Self-pity and bitterness had promised her that they would protect her from pain, they would hide her from anger, but they left her fragile and afraid. Walking with her dogs to the river and through the neighborhood brought her peace. During these times she would often whisper prayers to Mulungu or sing songs to Yesu. She would cry and give Him her heartache and grief. She would always start out sad but, by the time she got back, she would be filled with hope and peace.

As the years progressed, hatred brought a new enemy: confusion. Now Bahati wore all black and gray to cover up the wonderful colors she felt inside. The colors of her heart could not find their way to the surface because hatred had pushed them far back. Joy and laughter had left after she felt love turned its back on her, but she had turned her back on it. There was no beauty in the wilderness, flowers, or the colors of the soul. Just cement and stone brought comfort to Bahati. Cement and stone represented death, something she had tried to achieve, but Life rescued her from its claws.

Bahati left home and moved to a foreign land to go to college. She was far from the Ngong Hills where she had found solace during her walks with her pets. Now she was on her own, juggling existence past and present. She decided to travel to see her friends from secondary school. They had always helped her find purpose in life. Bahati had an acquaintance named Daniel. She called him Friendship, because he exuberated the qualities of a good friend, and she had prayed for one. She did not want a boyfriend, just a friend. She valued their bond. As she got older, she grew afraid of losing their friendship. Everyone seemed to have a boyfriend and she thought she needed one, too. It was not until years later, after she married, that she learned what was true love, and the difference between romantic and platonic love. She remembered, too, that she had asked Mulungu for a friend to get her through adolescent life, not a romantic boyfriend. She realized, years later, that because hatred had such a command on her heart, she could not attach to others and false love, with its lusts, easily filled her heart. At last Mulungu found a way in.

It was a cold evening as Bahati lay on the floor crying. Friendship, the doctor, and Friendship's family were kneeling over her. Bahati had tried to take her life, but Friendship stopped her. He helped Bahati remember the one thing that was more important to her in her life than false love: Mulungu. Though hatred had a grip on her heart, in that last moment Bahati remembered that love and compassion always hopes and never fails. Bahati thought, "Even if I can't feel love and compassion, I can hope and it won't fail me." Sure enough, Mulungu came through and Friendship walked into the room and halted her from taking her life that night. Friendship shared the Good Book with her, but Bahati turned it down for, even though she could breathe again, she was still not spiritually or emotionally alive. She had a long road back to real living.

After visiting with Friendship, Bahati went to visit her old schoolmate, Amita, who had always been a solid companion through secondary school. She called her Companionship. Bahati, weak from her battles with anger, bitterness, jealousy, and self-pity, was fragile. Her spirit was damaged and her soul could not fight hatred, even though she longed to be free of its grip. Then Companionship reminded Bahati of the two things that always made her strong: her faith in Mulungu and her love for Yesu. Though Companionship was East Indian, Bahati and her were life companions. They did not have to change themselves to be accepted by the other. They respected each other and knew what made the other strong. So, one day, Companionship told Bahati to go back to Mulungu and lay herself bare to Him. "Let His guides help you back." Bahati, still stubborn from hatred, fought back and said no. But then love began to push through and what little hope inside her heart remained said, "Try, just try." So Bahati went back to Mulungu and whispered a prayer. She told him about her hate, anger, self-pity, jealousy, bitterness, and fear. She was embarrassed to tell him about a new enemy, unfaithfulness; she never thought she would let it in, but she had. After she bared her soul to Mulungu, she lit a candle for hope. She left feeling lighter and freer. Her confidence was coming back and there was a smile on her face. It was a new beginning, and yet it was one of the first steps back to a loving and compassionate heart. She had many more steps to take.

Bahati arrived back home from her travels and visits with Friendship and Companionship. She remembered Companionship's last words to her: "Go back and be strong. Be strong for yourself; not for neediness, helplessness, or selfishness, but for you." On the ride back to the house from the airport, Bahati felt a new sense of adventure about where life was taking her. She was ready to try again, and she was done with hatred. However, hatred was going to fight for her spirit, soul, and mind. Bahati was stronger this time. She wanted to be close to Mulungu again, so she spent time reading the Good Book in old English, visiting Mulungu's house, and listening for His voice through His guides. One day, she was walking in the courtyard and came across two women who later became her friends, Janice and Ruth. Bahati named them Innocence and Honesty, for they both exuded these inner qualities. They offered her friendship and a chance to read the Good Book to learn more about love and the way to true living. Bahati was enthralled. She had always read about people who followed Yesu with a learner's heart, but she had not seen many living in the twenty-first century. She was inspired that Ruth, whom she called Innocence, and Janice, whom she referred to as Honesty, were not counterfeit. They were honest about their shortcomings and lived to fight hatred and its lies. Bahati could not believe how brave they were. Their lives were inspiring to watch, so she listened to what Mulungu had to say in his Good Book about life, love, second chances, and honor.

Bahati would walk about five miles to get to Innocence and Honesty's house to read about Mulungu. She was inspired to learn from young women who had graduated college and begun their careers as professionals. When they began to read the Good Book, Bahati felt a fire burn in her heart as she read the pages. At times, she felt also a willful urge to close the book and walk out the door. Occasionally she would send a critical eye to Honesty and Innocence. She was looking for any lack of virtue as she felt threatened by their inner strength. Sometimes she felt her mind swimming with confusion and her chest tighten as she struggled with onus over her thoughts toward Innocence and Honesty. On the days when the feelings of onus were strongest, Bahati would feel like cutting herself, not combing her hair, and not going out of the house. Onus would take on its own persona and overcome Bahati's weak soul. Bahati had not yet learned to control her spirit, so it went every which way it desired. But Honesty and Innocence were stronger than Bahati's onus, especially Honesty. Honesty would say, "That's right, that's me, but love found a way for me to change. Love can help you too." Honesty always showed Bahati the freedom that honesty itself offers the human being.

For most of her life, Bahati had tried to be perfect and live a life of perfection, but imperfection was reality. No matter how many good deeds she did to try to make up for her imperfection, onus laid a heavy load on her shoulders. Innocence taught her how she could obtain innocence even though she was imperfect. Mulungu had a simple plan for people, but many of us don't want it. Bahati, too, did not want it for a long time. Then she realized that with love and through Yesu, she could be honest and innocent. Perfection had been realized. Yet Bahati had further to go. Why did she want so much to be perfect? So much of it was because jealousy and self-pity had taught her to compete with other people. She was not the smartest, fastest, prettiest, tallest, or kindest, but she thought she could be the most obedient. Innocence and Honesty had her read what Mulungu taught on obedience and she found Mulungu's greatest hope: if she could love Him and others, that would be enough. Wow! Bahati was at the bottom of the pile again. She had spent so much time hating, how could she now love greatly? Yet, now that she knew what perfection was, would she choose innocence and truth? Would she admit that she was unloving, but loved by Mulungu? Would she accept Mulungu's love or keep her false sense of perfection? The choice was hers to make, but she was afraid because her last chip of self-armor was coming down. She would be bare before Mulungu and the world, and only grace and truth could lift her up and give her confidence, if she believed.

Innocence and Honesty looked at Bahati and told her, "We cannot force you. It is your choice. It is your decision to make." Bahati said, "I don't know." The room went silent, the Good Book was closed, and Bahati felt alone at the crossroads. Innocence and Honesty had shared grace and truth with her, but now Bahati had to choose if she wanted grace and truth for herself. Innocence and Honesty, no matter how much they wanted to cover Bahati's bareness before the truth of who she really was, could not. Bahati would have to choose either hatred or love for clothing. However, the only way love could cover her again, as it did when she was a child, was through sincerity and purity. Bahati would have to spend a little time with Yesu to get the courage to be personally honest and innocent about who she was before humanity and Mulungu.

The next twenty-four hours were a battle in Bahati's mind. Hatred has many ways of manifesting itself, including through cold, calculated thought. Bahati loved to think and analyze things in her mind. There she was safe to ponder, discover, and wonder. But love was so much simpler and more humble. "Just be you," she could hear her heart beat. But her mind demanded proof and understanding for this love. This went on for hours, and then Bahati's soul broke free. Her thoughts were clear. "No, I did choose bitterness and to despise others. Yes, I did choose these emotions and feelings. Yes, I do believe love was sacrificed for me so I could overcome bitterness and love again. Yes, I do want to love again. I do want to come home, Mulungu." In that moment, Bahati felt confident. She was focused and, though afraid, she was strong. The next day she stood at the water, just like the river she had walked to with Kidogo, Kwezi, Karen, and Getta as a troubled adolescent girl. This time though she was not going across the river, but underneath the water. Here she would experience the power of grace and truth freeing her from the grip of the anger she had embraced in her adolescence. As she came up out of the river she could see and feel again in living and loving color. Her heart felt warm as she smiled at Innocence and Honesty. She even gave them a big hug and did not feel awkward about it. She felt calm and peaceful inside. Bahati realized that, this time, peace was going to last more than a moment, prayer, or a walk. This time she would breathe again in her soul, and the breath in her would overcome her inner struggles with animosity, lust, jealousy, bitterness, self-pity, and fear. This time she would live the power of love over perfection, the power of a relationship created by sincerity and purity. Bahati decided she would choose emotional intimacy over rules and regulations. This time she would experience the rewards of love and true confidence. Bahati would walk again in her soul and, in time learn to run, and soar later like Life's eagles. This time Bahati would be free! So Bahati decided to stick with grace and truth. Bahati chose compassion, love, and truth over perfection. Compassion, love, and truth had won—they just needed the help of bravery. Would Bahati be brave? Yes, with the help of wisdom and love itself, she would.

VIGNETTE NUMBER FIVE
A Man and Woman Worthy of Honor

The Heartbeat of Africa

Weeping, falling tears of every man,
woman, and child.
Can we hear them? Do we want to hear them?
No, we are too far away in our personal worlds
with our fancy cars and MTV.

Well they're weeping still,
And their blood is flowing down our
Indifference.

And I am weeping from within,
Trying to get out,
Trying to express the pain, the anguish,
the despair of my Fellow man.

Susu's weeping because there is no need
for her in this modern world.

Umau's weeping because he has lost his eldership role to
education. The traditional ways hold no meaning anymore.

And darkness is weeping.
Ssh! Ssh!

Listen to the moans of the night.
Listen to hope scream in agony as it loses its Life
And fire consumes us all.

We have no tomorrow because we have
abandoned yesterday's lessons.
We no longer listen for the ancestor's voice.

Yet hope remains! Those of us who will listen to the Stories of
our elders will live to tell those stories to our children.

Then each of us will go on, and Africa itself will go on.

We rarely remember those who have walked before us these days!
So many steps ahead we all say we must climb. Tomorrow circumvents
yesterday. Tomorrow is more important. What can the past teach us?
What can our ancestors teach us? Tomorrow brings hope, we say,
but little do we know that tomorrow brings a repeat of yesterday's
yesterday. Our ancestors, our history, our yesterday, they are all there
to tell us how to live today, and hopefully tomorrow, if we will only
listen to their voices. The voices of the trees, birds, air, and, yes, the
voices of our ancestors all call out. Do we hear them offer proverbs
and parables of wisdom for today's dilemmas?

But today, tonight, we take a look back at a man and woman
worthy of honor. They came from their own ancestors, who came
from their own, who came from the soil in their Creator's hands.
Like their ancestors, they have returned to the soil, and I will join
them, but will their voices remain?

Bahati sits by her window so far from Lang'ata in a foreign land,
feeling the cold night breeze come through the window. She remembers the day she stood by the corner window in the kitchen in
her home in Lang'ata. She remembers that window clearly because it
was made from a special glass and had a small crack in it. From the
window she could see where her father lay with his family, friends,
and neighbors, for the last time. She remembers her mother sitting

by his casket with the warmth of friends, family, and the community all around. Bahati searches back to find her father in her memories. She searches through old photos to find the home she grew up in, to find the window that she stood in when she saw him for the last time. And, in one moment, she feels him compelling her to go forward; to love the man Mulungu gave her, to embrace her husband, and to go forward and build a better world for her family and Humanity, as Mulungu and her ancestors would want her to do. She can hear her dad telling her, "Run, run, run forward and don't look back." In that quiet moment, she realizes he is not back in the old house. He is in her heart and in all the hearts of those who love him. She realizes he is Mulungu's voice calling her to keep moving forward to keep loving Love and humanity. Bahati realizes she must go on. Looking back will not bring her father back, but going forward will give him the honor she so longs to give him today, tonight. She surrenders and whispers *Hallelujah! Hallelujah!*

She has one picture left that hangs in her hallway. He was a great man with great dreams who died too young with a bride so devoted and loyal through all the hard times, until his moment of departure. All this Bahati remembers as she thinks back to the day she looked out of that kitchen window in her Lang'ata home so many years ago. Around her, her aunties and cousins were preparing food for the guests, but Bahati stood at a distance, curious. How would she go on, knowing that she would never hear her father's voice again, smell his scent, or look into his stern eyes? This permanent change came from one phone call, one specific telegram from her uncle, "Come home father is gone." And, in that moment, she knew life would never be the same; she felt as though a covering had been lifted off her shoulder. She would have to protect her family and herself now. She would have to trust in Mulungu to rescue her from hard times now, because her dad was no longer there. Oh! The strength fathers provide us. Let us all say thank you while we can, while there is breath in our lungs and air in our mouths to whisper the sounds. Let them know, let them live with confidence and breathe their last breaths with hope.

Twenty-two years passed, but Mulungu has a way of hearing our cries, and one day Bahati found an old record of her father's voice. As the days built up to her receiving the album by her father and hearing his voice for the first time since their last phone call, her heart beat fast. She did not know what to expect; would he be stern as she remembered him in her youth? Would he have a baritone voice? Who was he? It had been twenty-two years since she last heard his voice before he parted from those who loved him most.

When the album arrived, for the first few seconds she could not hear the father she knew. This man was so tender. Then she realized that the sternness was to hide the fear. As she listened more, she could hear him. He always ended his sentences with a point. He wanted his listener to understand. As she listened again and again, she could hear him, and from here she will tell his story, the story of a man and woman of honor.

Bahati's father had been born into a humble family in Kibwezi, Kenya. He was an explorer and found his way, one day, on the newly created British railroad track and train in Uganda. There he worked as a houseboy for some time before returning to his hometown. When he returned, he heard his siblings speaking an unknown language and wanted to learn it. It was English. Soon, he was excelling in a missionary school and eventually traveled across the sea to the United States to obtain his master's degree. He worked hard while he was in college and had a local job, a radio show, and attended his graduate classes. It was in the United States that he met his devoted friend and later wife, Mary. She left everything she knew to join him in Kenya after the completion of their graduate and undergraduate degrees. Bahati's father always had a fire in him to return home and rebuild his country. He was a generous man, and his home was always filled with relatives or individuals who needed support and education. Over the years, several relatives, who later became doctors or went on to raise their own families and educate them overseas, lived in their home. Bahati recalls her uncle who became a doctor and another who became a pilot. She always thinks of this when it is her turn to lend a hand to others. She remembers her father and mother's example. If they had not opened their home, given money, taught English lessons, or simply listened, so many people may not have had the opportunity to achieve their dreams.

Bahati was just a young child when her father, Amani, first arrived in Nairobi and went to work as the chief buyer of a local manufacturing company. However, his desire to help his people out of poverty superseded his desire to become individually wealthy. Amani would often make trips to Kibwezi and Machakos to help with fundraisers to build schools, shops, or other infrastructure that would help the Akamba people. The Ambua clan elders soon elevated him to a leader in the community, as he was wise and generous. They provided him with a three-pronged stool, which was carved and made specifically for him. He was very proud of this stool. Bahati's family still has it.

Amani soon decided to leave his managerial job and pursue a career as a member of parliament. He believed he could do more for the people as a member of parliament. The next few years were a struggle for him as he fought the establishment on behalf of the people. Amani was not overcome by his wealth and always remembered where he had come from. He wanted the opportunities he had to be available to the Kamba people. The establishment, however, enjoyed the status quo and the wealth they had obtained after independence. Greed looks the same wherever you go.

Whenever he left Nairobi and went up country, the children and villagers would run to meet him. Bahati remembers one visit they made to Kibwezi. Her father had gathered the people together to help raise money to build a school. Hundreds of people had gathered together in a local church building. The crowd grew and later spilled out into the street. Bahati watched as the people followed and leaned on every word her father said. However, she noticed that, though they loved him, it was not enough for change. At election time, no matter how many supporters Amani had going into an election, the peoples' vote could be dissuaded with a meal of chicken and rice.

Tonight, as Bahati sits in her home, she thinks that this seems like such a trivial thing, but she recalls world history and current events, and remembers people are fickle, including herself. She recalls in the book of Matthew, how everyone was rejoicing over Yesu and then in just a few chapters, they were all shouting to crucify him.

Bahati took a deep breath, "I wish we all were not so fickle. I wish I was not fickle, but this is man, and if you want to change things, you have to be strong because change does not come easy." Yet her father had made a difference. At his funeral were people from every walk of life: East Indian, Kikuyu, Kamba, British, and, of course, his family. He had made a change. He had brought people from different walks of life together. This was an amazing scene to Bahati, with all these people showing their respect. She realized her father wanted to help people out of poverty, but what people needed so much more was his compassion, and in the end they honored him for this.

Alongside his casket sat his wife, Mary. She was faithful and loyal. When she left the United States, she had just gained several freedoms through civil rights. She moved to an underdeveloped country that was just gaining its independence from the British Empire. She left behind driving her car and wearing her miniskirt, to live in a country where women did not know how to drive and certainly did not wear miniskirts. She had a long cultural battle before her, but she stood by Amani. She did not leave him no matter how hard it was for her at times. She was a classroom teacher at an elementary school and later at a secretarial school, even though she had a bachelor's degree from a renowned university. She later developed several farming projects that led to small businesses.

Amani and she were both industrious and used their degrees to the fullest. They built apartments for people to live in on another side of town, and started a printing business. They taught their children to recycle and compost long before recycling was a popular idea. They grew organic fruits and vegetables on their ten-acre farm and raised farm animals, which they lived off of until the day Amani died and Mary returned to the United States. Amani was interested in solar power back in the 80s, and installed solar panels on their Lang'ata home's rooftop so that they could have hot water and reduce the electric bill. Amani built a tank to hold water that they collected from the river flowing through their property. They used the water in the tank to irrigate their farm. Yes, Mary and Amani were not only friends and husband and wife, they were also entrepreneurs.

Mary had been born to a Native American father and African American mother. Her father had built the house they lived in. Mary lived before the civil rights movement and experienced many injustices. One such example was going to a restaurant with her father, who was much lighter skinned than she and her mother. As a result, her mother and Mary had to wait outside because they were black. It is amazing that even though she endured these racial injustices, she did not let them divide her love for her father who was privileged in the United States.

Mary excelled in school, becoming "Who's Who" in high school and later being accepted to a renowned university. Her mother worked hard at the local naval base as a house cleaner. Her family had strong ethics and worked hard. During the civil rights, Mary was active in the movement and developed many scars. When documentaries would come on television, Mary would share her civil rights stories with Bahati and her siblings.

Mary and Amani, however, faced their own struggles as a bi-cultural couple. Mary had to resist many stereotypes about not being Akamba, and Amani had to explain why he had not married an Akamba woman. Even through these difficult years, they stood by each other. The fruit of their union was definitely their children, but Bahati's cousin Mumbua was their prize. Mumbua was the daughter of a relative of Amani. Mumbua was a bright child and wanted desperately to learn. Mary had compassion for her and brought her to their home. She taught Mumbua as much as she knew and Mumbua blossomed as much as she could. Mumbua had her struggles in life, but later grew to be a strong businesswoman, forever grateful to Mary and Amani for giving her the chance to learn about the world.

After Amani's passing, Mary returned to the United States. She had to start from scratch. Her hometown had changed and she did not recognize it anymore. She carried the wounds of life, but also the strength of her father, who had built her home when she was a child and the heartbeat of her mother, who had lived through the Great Depression. Mary worked hard and did what she could to love those around her. As a single parent, it was a struggle, but she did her best and provided for her family.

Tonight in her apartment, Bahati listens to the music in her CD player and remembers life is but a breath, and looking back on faults or criticizing the weak will not make them strong. Love must find its way and the good must outshine our human faults, as we all have them.

Bahati listens once more to her father's voice on the album. She can't believe that it took twenty-two years for her to appreciate and find his voice. He was a gentle man and a kind man. Life was hard on him, so he was sometimes hard on life. However, tonight she can hear the gentle man as he speaks so clearly through the album. Bahati can hear his youth. His dreams had just begun; he was just about to return to Kenya, not knowing what lay ahead of him and his family. He had the confidence of a young idealist leader, hope punctuated at the end of every sentence. In his voice she heard his plans for Kenya, his plans for the Akamba people, his plans for the Ambua clan, his plans for his siblings and parents, and his plans for his wife and children. And so he continued, each sentence stronger than the last with the confidence of a young man who knows he will make a difference. A young man who has overcome poverty, language barriers, racism, and life itself to not only tell his story, but build up a nation. A nation he saw gain its independence with his own eyes. Bahati remembers those fiery eyes and for a moment realizes that the fire was not just anger or frustration, but it was zeal and passion to see the phoenix rise from the ashes. Amani had seen it happen in his own life and he was certain it could happen for his countrymen, his tribe, his brother, and his children. These were the eyes destined to help build a nation that needed building. He could have chosen so many paths. He could have stayed in the United States and become wealthy, but he chose to go back home, to give it all up to help his fellow man reach his full potential. What selflessness, what desire, what hope!

Now twenty-two years later, Bahati thought, Life gives and it takes. Each breath, each day, something given and something taken. It matters how we live, it matters what our last breath will bring. Will it bring us peace or will it bring us regret? Will it give others life and love, or will it take from them their last hope? Yes how we live matters.

Amani and Mary live on in many ways. Will Bahati listen to her ancestors and elders? Will we listen to them calling from their graves, calling in the night, calling out from yesterday, "Young man, woman, don't go this way, go that; take this turn, not that"? Will we listen or are we busy climbing tomorrow's hill, tomorrow's journey, and tomorrow's ambition? Too fast to stop and listen to the trees, birds, air, and, yes, our ancestors saying, "Take this road, young man, woman, it leads to life worth living." She can hear her father say, "Remember Mulungu, the Great I Am, in all your ways! He will straighten out the road ahead of you, my daughter, and guard your steps. Remember Bahati! Remember! Always Remember! So, though Amani and Mary are not fundraising in Kibwezi or building schools in Machakos, Amani's voice continues, and Bahati is here to tell the story of a man and woman worthy of honor.

VIGNETTE NUMBER SIX
All Alone in the Big City

In the past, many people who lived at the foot of the Ngong Hills left their towns, villages, and homes where they had grown up. Some moved to the big city, while some moved to foreign cities to attend college and find jobs. Those who had the opportunity to go to foreign lands have many untold stories of their travels and life experiences, like Bahati. She left her village to live in a big city that was mountains, rivers, lakes, and oceans away from her home in Lang'ata at the foot of the Ngong Hills. Her father had passed away, and she felt further from her emotional base than ever before. She treasured her memories while she lived in the big city amidst skyscrapers and many unfamiliar faces. These memories prepared Bahati for a space for her to enter into emotionally, where she could find true love just around the corner and for the first time.

Bahati was in Form 5 when most of her friends began to leave Kenya and go to school in Europe and America. She had just completed her O' Level exams and was distraught. While she had studied and worked for a Division 1, she had only scored a Division 3. The school she went to was considered affluent, and she had heard that the examiners had graded her school, and others like it, with a keen and disapproving eye. The tide was changing for the privileged, and people were looking for a way out from under the weight of corruption.

Bahati's family was very involved in the community and, though she went to a privileged school, her father made her siblings and her work in the shamba—the farm—during holidays. Bahati had been to Mombasa only once and was often embarrassed by her father's refusal to buy a fancy car like the other children's parents at her school. He loved his 1970s Peugeot, which often broke down in the middle of the road. Bahati's father believed that success was in the land and not in material things. Bahati remembered this life lesson in the big city. Like her father, she bought few things so that she was always able to lend a hand to someone in need. Later, as she got to know her Grandma Berry, who had lived in the city all her life, she learned how to live on even less. Grandma Berry had lived through the Great Depression and understood what it was like to save so you could have a little to share tomorrow.

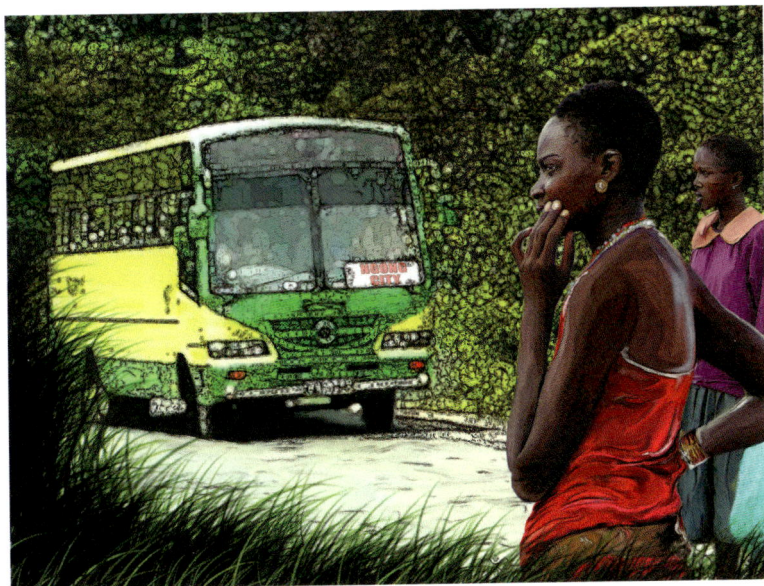

Bahati Watching Bus Go

Now, all grown up and in a foreign city, on many occasions Bahati would find herself lonely and daydreaming of home. She missed Kidogo, Kwezi, Karen, and Getta, her favorite pets who brought her much comfort. She missed her long walks to the river and through her neighborhood, but most of all she missed the Ngong Hills. "Oh!

How I long for the Ngong Hills," she would think. "Oh! How I used to sit and peer out of my window and watch the butterflies dance in the sunset and listen to the birds sing as the sun rose each morning. Oh! Ngong Hills, how I long for you in this wild and busy city. My heart still beats for you as I ponder the peace you brought me as a young girl."

Bahati with Butterfly

One day, when Bahati returned from work in the big city, she sat on her bed and recalled her many trips with her family to visit her grandparents in Kibwezi and, later, Machakos. The Mombasa highway was a long stretch of paved road that passed by Machakos, Kibwezi, and Tsavo. Bahati remembered the scenes of rolling hills, thorn trees, and savannah along the highway. Sometimes, on the long drive from Nairobi to Kibwezi, she would see impalas, zebu cows, and a few zebra grazing on the savannah. She often pondered about the time it took to get there as she stared at the savannah from the backseat window of her father's white Peugeot. Bahati remembered how the terrain changed the closer they got to Kibwezi. The soil turned red and dusty. She recalls this clearly, because they would turn off the Mombasa highway and take the dirt roads to her grandparents' house. The vegetation was less luscious in these parts,

Susu with grandchildren

the baobab trees were thick with their branches pointing upward, and it was very hot. The car would always come to a stop outside a tin-roofed house that her father had built for his parents. This image somehow stopped Bahati in her thoughts!

She had arrived, in her mind, at Susu's door. She began to contemplate to herself, "I remember how Susu would gather Mwikali, Mutuku, and me together at night to tell us stories." She recalled speaking Kiswahili with Susu, as she did not speak Kikamba, her father's native tongue. Years later, Bahati would regret not sticking through her Kikamba language classes, which her parents had established for her to learn Kikamba. In actual truth she was never really good with any language. Mothers in the Akamba tribe do a lot of the child rearing and pass on their mother tongue to their children. Bahati's mother taught her English. Her mother learned Swahili as well and assisted in Bahati speaking this with her relatives. Back at Susu's door, Bahati remembered how Susu enlightened Mwikali, Mutuku, and her about Mulungu.

Susu told them legends of the great warriors of Kenya, like Muindi wa Mbingu. She told tales of how the hyena got its spots. All these things Bahati remembered and treasured in her heart. As the evening went on, Bahati remembered the very night Susu told her how Mulungu used his imagination to create the world. Susu described how Mulungu breathed warmth into his creation and filled our hearts with love. Susu told her, "Mulungu gave us tranquility and peace like the waters of Lake Nyanza. His love reaches beyond the snow-topped peaks of Mount Kilimanjaro and Mount Kenya, and his compassion fills the depths of the Indian Ocean."

Susu told Bahati that Mulungu created the world because He wanted to provide good things to all humankind through laughter, showers of rain, and land to walk and rest upon. Susu reminded Mutuku, Mwikali, and Bahati that the warmth of Mulungu's love surrounds us as the equator encircles the earth. "His love gives light to illuminate the boundaries He has set for us to live." At that moment Bahati recalled a particular juncture when her family and she traveled home from one of their trips to visit Susu and Umau in Kibwezi. On this specific occasion, her father had to stop the car because the sun was setting horizontally on the equator and they could not see past the brilliant light. As her Susu spoke that night, the moon shone brighter than it ever did before and all the stars hung brightly around it. It was as though Mulungu was showing them his glory.

Now alone in the big city among the busy streets, bustling city sounds, and tall skyscrapers, Bahati was far from her family and the Ngong Hills. Bahati cried herself into a deep, deep sleep and dreamed of home. In her dream she saw her family, the Ngong Hills, and her Susu. Susu looked into her eyes and wiped away her tears. She said, "Our Mulungu never leaves us though we sometimes leave Him. He never goes away though we sometimes lose heart because of life's trials. Though we lose our childlike faith, He is always here. Do not cry, though you may feel all alone in the city, for Mulungu lives! He lives to bring you comfort and compassion when you need Him most. He is with us in the peaks and valleys of life."

Mount Kilimanjaro

Bahati stirred in her sleep and awoke from her dream. She looked around the room. Had Susu come to comfort her and console her? Her heart filled with joy at the thought of it, and she went to the window and peered out at the stars and moon. In a whispered prayer she said, "Mulungu, I have lost my trust and hope amid the skyscrapers and busy streets of this wild and bustling city. Please show me your glory, as you did in my youth, and make my hard heart soft again. Then the love in my heart will flow free with time, just as the river Tana flows freely downstream into the Indian Ocean. I will know that all that Susu said was true, and I will cry no more."

River Tana

At that, the clouds moved away from the moon and the stars shone brightly in the sky. A star shone so brightly that its glorious light pierced Bahati's heart, and she began to sing softly to Mulungu. As she sang, her heart grew softer and softer, until she could hear her heartbeat and see the joy of her soul illuminated on her face through the bedroom window. Her tears of joy trickled down her face, and in a quiet whisper, Bahati said, "Mulungu, you are truly there though the darkness hides thee."

VIGNETTE NUMBER SEVEN
Poke and Chumvi

To My Loving Blossom

Wisdom from afar
grows in an early spring rain
seeing it change me.
The Cherry Blossoms
fragile and very beautiful
will last but a day.
How little I know
but Kami-sama has so much wisdom;
please help me find some.
Are you listening?
Hoping, praying, wanting truth
and finding them in Kami-sama.
A friend who loves you
cares deeply, willing to risk
everything for love.
He longs for your answer.
It's your turn—are you ready?
But what will it be...
Together better with Kami-sama
Nothing can stop us.
Please be my love.

Bahati finally grew up and married. Tonight, she takes a deep breath and watches her husband, Isamu, wrestle in his sleep. "Thank you, Mulungu, for bringing him into my life and letting me become his wife," she thinks. Poke, as she likes to call him because he loves people and fish, is resting from a long workday. Chumvi, Poke's nickname for Bahati because he said she brought seasoning into his life, is remembering that it has been a few years since their two paths crossed and they married. "I was in such a hurry to get to the top, and he, such a humble man," Bahati thought. "At first, I thought our two groups' heritages would separate us." After all, it was a known fact that Asians and blacks did not get along together. But her friend from college, Little Brother, as Bahati liked to call him, was wise. He was Asian, too, so he was qualified to offer wisdom on the situation. He had known Bahati for several years during college and was a loyal friend. Not many people have friends who look out for them and help them find a spouse, but Little Brother did. He had seen Bahati broken, year after year, as she was disappointed by romantic crushes. Now that he himself was married, he finally stepped up and said, "Bahati, let me introduce you to someone with whom you can build a loving relationship and friendship."

As the day approached for Bahati and Isamu's first date, Bahati began to doubt and become uncertain. She was afraid her heart would be broken again. After all, she was so much older now, and it had not worked out so many times before. In fact, Bahati had several crushes and one emotional friendship that had lasted across three continents and never materialized into anything substantial. So, technically, Bahati was a middle-aged woman who had never had a boyfriend. She was awkward, socially and in relationships. She had never learned to feel comfortable around the opposite gender. She always felt she could not keep a conversation without seeming weird and, if she did like someone, she lacked prudence and would find herself stargazing into the person's eyes. So Bahati was very nervous about her first date with Isamu. Would she like him? Would he like

her? How would she know if he liked her? How would she find out
if he liked her? When would she see him again if she liked him?
All these questions, and others, raced through her mind. It was not
until years later that Bahati learned Isamu's confidence, how to be
in the moment and not have the moment take over you. She arrived
early at Little Brother and his wife's house. Shortly thereafter, Isamu
arrived. Bahati thought he was handsome with a kind, spirited face.
He had a gentle voice, smooth skin, and a brilliant smile, but more
importantly he listened when she spoke. Bahati spoke quietly to
Kalama, Little Brother's wife, and said, "I can tell he is listening
because he does not just hold his tongue, but he also acknowledges
my words, especially when I speak of the pain in my heart. He is
not scared of me. I am not strange to him. What a kind soul behind
those dark eyes." That night, Poke did a lot of listening, but later
in their friendship he spoke and did not stop speaking and telling
Chumvi his feelings, thoughts, hopes, and dreams.

That night, as Isamu slept by her side, Bahati pulled out the
poem that Isamu wrote to ask her to become his girlfriend. What
wonder, what gentleness, and what tenderness. "You don't usually
find these qualities in a man," she thinks to herself. Isamu had them
and yet he was strong, a Samurai in his own right, who could defend
a king's heart, soul, and body. He had studied Wado-Ryu under a
sensei who studied under the founder of this martial art. Isamu
earned his black belt, yet he did not use his might to teach others
to hurt. Like the style itself, he taught others to care for each other,
despite their differences, and gain inner self-control. He worked
every weekend with his friends to train children on how to gain self-
control through martial arts. He taught children, regardless of their
ability, how to understand each other and how to hold themselves
together through life. Yes, tonight Bahati thinks back to those first
dates and even heartbreaks that they shared.

Bahati and Isamu dated for several months during the early
spring, summer, and fall. When the winter came, Isamu's heart
grew cold with pain. He had lost a lot in his life and desired to be

alone. Bahati could not understand why he was shutting her out. She was hurt. Later she would learn that emotional closeness was something Isamu feared. Bahati recalls the day she came home from work and her roommate, Olivia, took her aside and told her that Isamu's friend, Isaiah, had called to tell her that Isamu said he was not interested in building a relationship. Bahati was crushed. She had hoped and Little Brother had promised, but now she was back where she had always been—alone and hurt, not fully understanding why. A friend Mark who she named Understanding, because he had great perception into the hearts of men and women, encouraged her not to focus on the obvious and to attempt to understand what was really going on for Isamu. Bahati did not want to do this. "Why should I care for someone who does not care for me?" she asked. Understanding responded, "Because caring itself is reward enough." Bahati was silent. This was a message of Yesu, loving just to love without wanting anything back in return. Bahati struggled with this, as her heart had a history of giving into bitterness and self-pity. It was hard to love just to love and expect nothing in return. It was hard just to hope for hope's sake, to give for giving's sake, and to believe for faith's sake. But she did. Bahati believed and did not harden her heart. As always, Mulungu came through as He does when we hold true to love. Soon enough, Isamu was asking Bahati on a date. Isamu called, "Hi, Bahati, how are you? I was wondering if you would like to go out on a date?" Bahati thought to herself, "Is he crazy? No explanation for the long silence?" but she answered "Yes," and so they went on that date that led to the beginning of their forever after.

Isamu picked Bahati up and took her to a nice restaurant out of town. During the meal, he began to talk about all the wonderful gifts he had received from different people he had dated. Bahati was baffled. "He can't be serious," she thought. "First silence, now this. Does he like me or not?" Bahati pretended to listen, and then her jealousy kicked in. She pretended that she did not care, but when the date ended, Bahati went home with a heavy heart.

The next day Isamu called Bahati. They exchanged small talk for a while, and then Bahati just asked Isamu straight up, "What are your motives?"

Isamu was silent for a second. "Well, I like you Bahati!" Bahati's heart was racing with joy, and then she heard the next line, "But there are so many others to choose from."

Bahati did not know what to say. In one way she was glad that Isamu trusted her enough to be honest with her. No other gentleman had. On the other hand, the truth was hard to hear. Bahati took a silent breath, and then responded, "Well, Isamu you will have to choose. I am older now and my heart has been broken many times. I cannot walk between cold and hot paths. I cannot be lukewarm."

Isamu was silent on the other end of the phone, and then he said, "Okay, I will have to get back to you." Bahati was saddened in that moment that Isamu did not have an answer then and there, but at the same time she was glad that the truth was out. No more games, no more guesses, but was she ready to hear his answer? Was she ready to hear him say no? She had heard this so many times and her heart was not sure she could hear it again, but the truth was better than pretending. They talked for a few minutes about life and work and then hung up the phone. Bahati looked straight ahead, and there she could see herself in the mirror. A brown-skinned Ambua woman! Her hair was braided, intertwined with extensions and pulled back into a bun. Her brown eyes were slightly slanted from her ancestral genes and her lips were shaped like apple slices. Her nose seemed like a stubby little ski jump, and her cheekbones protruded but were not high enough to notice. Would anyone choose her? Would anyone love her? This was a question she had asked herself over and over again throughout her life, and now, looking into the mirror, she took a short but deep breath. She knew Mulungu would love her, and she would await Isamu's answer.

Two weeks rolled by and Bahati had heard no word from Isamu. Her faith was dry, and she was ready to turn to her old ways of bitterness and loneliness. Then she talked with Understanding, her friendly guide. Understanding reminded her that one does not lose when they love someone else and it is not reciprocated. The person is refreshed by love itself. Understanding reminded her that patience was key and helped her consider what Isamu may be experiencing. Perhaps Isamu was afraid, perhaps he was baffled, perhaps he did not want to be rejected, perhaps he did not want to be abandoned, and perhaps he, too, had something to lose in all of this. Bahati had never considered love from the other person's perspective. She was always afraid of being rejected because that was all she had experienced. She was afraid of being known and then disliked. She had never thought about the other person, that perhaps he had scars and fears, perhaps he did not comprehend his own feelings and emotions, or perhaps he, too, needed to be loved just for love's sake. Yes! Understanding taught Bahati to wait patiently and to believe in True Love, and Love itself.

Olivia came up to Bahati to comfort her as she waited to hear from Isamu. "It has been a few weeks, has it not?" she said to Bahati.

"Yes, it has."

Olivia took Bahati's hand and said, "Let's take a walk down by the water. It will soothe your soul. It always does." They put on their coats and went down by the water. The sun was setting and it was a little chilly. Bahati whispered a prayer and then they sang. Suddenly Bahati noticed she heard only her voice. Olivia was not singing. She opened her eyes, for she had closed them to take in the evening air and focus on Mulungu's love. When she turned around Isamu was standing behind her holding a dozen roses. Bahati was baffled. Her head was spinning. She had set emotionally with the sunset, and now, with Isamu standing there with a dozen roses, she felt her heart rising in her soul. Her head was dizzy with emotion, and she could barely hear Isamu say, "I have a message for you." Then he began to read the poem he had written for her.

Wisdom from afar
grows in an early spring
seeing it change me
The cherry blossoms
fragile and very beautiful
will last but a day.
How little I know
but Kami-sama has so much wisdom
please help me find some.
Are you listening
hoping, praying, wanting truth
finding them in Kami-sama
A friend who loves you
cares deeply, willing to risk
everything for love.
He longs your answer
It's your turn, are you ready
but what will it be....
Together better
with Kami-sama, nothing can stop us
please be my girlfriend.

"Yes! I mean, what are you doing here? Where did you come from?" Bahati asked. She was lost for words. Then, out of the clearing, Peter and Chikae came up and joined Olivia, Isamu, and Bahati. Everyone was laughing. Chikae, who was also Japanese like Isamu, was so excited to be there and witness this special moment. Bahati was still confused. It all happened so fast. Then, Isamu told her that they had dinner plans and were going to go and meet up with Little Brother, his wife, Kalama, and their other friends. Bahati went home and noticed the cherry blossom tree was in full bloom outside her living room window. She called her mother. "Mom, I have a boyfriend." Bahati had waited many years to say that. Her mother was thrilled that her daughter had found love, and they laughed together on the phone. Then Peter, Chikae, Olivia, Isamu, and Bahati all got in the car and left for sushi at a restaurant in the city.

Isamu and Bahati dated for a few years and grew in their friendship and love for each other. Bahati sometimes had her doubts because they were so different. Isamu was a kind and modest man, and she an ambitious woman who sometimes did not know when to stop developing her next project. Bahati was a worldly woman, even though she fought to be spiritual. Her ambition always pulled her away from her humanity and faith. Isamu, on the other hand, not only understood humanity, he also epitomized it in his very being. He could overlook an offense, not engage a proud man, ignore a rude one, and he knew how to help friends overcome their differences. Bahati could see that Kami-sama (Mulungu) honored Isamu and lifted him up by giving him eternal riches, riches that do not run out. Bahati made her choice it would take some years of courtship for her to truly humble herself before Mulungu in order for Isamu to ask for her hand in marriage.

Then, one day Isamu took Bahati to one of her favorite prayer spots above the ocean floor, got down on one knee and asked her to marry him. She was excited. This time she was waiting patiently for the question and was grateful when he placed the engagement ring on her finger. She had never anticipated something so unique and brilliant. They went to dinner with their friends and then joined others at an engagement party. It was a joyous occasion filled with love and faith. Mrs. Young had driven down the coast to be with them. Even though she was well into her 70s, she had made the one-hour drive to be with Bahati. It was a day to remember. Bahati could feel the love in her heart for the first time as she looked at the balloons, cards, well wishes, and the engagement ring on her left hand.

In the months leading up to the wedding, Bahati found herself uneasy. Isamu and she did not have a lot of money saved for the wedding. She wanted Isamu to take on a second job to help raise money for the wedding, but her good, wise friend, Naomi, told her, "Your wedding day is one day, your marriage is a lifetime. How you build today will affect how your marriage withstands tomorrow's storms as a married couple." Bahati could not deny the wisdom in what she heard, so she reluctantly insisted that Isamu not take on that second job and that he focus his heart on Kami-sama, the children in his sports program, and his work. This was a hard decision to make, and one day she discovered why. She read *Akamba Stories* by Mbiti. She read the section on weddings and she remembered attending her cousin's wedding in Kenya when she was younger. Then it hit her: the man in the Kamba culture was to fight for the woman by buying her from her family. This was a sign of love. Bahati realized that she had two struggles in her: one, she did not feel loved, and, two, would her father, though deceased, be proud of the way she was being taken in hand? Bahati had to struggle one more time with Mulungu to find solace before she could marry Isamu with faith.

Bahati remembered the wedding of her cousin Miriam, an Ambua clanswoman, and the daughter of a famous military officer. Her father had promised her hand in marriage to Kimatu. She was afraid, but she proudly embraced the plan for her life. Bahati recalled as a young adolescent going to Miriam's home near Machakos and attending a large party for the couple. There were Kambas of all walks of life: rich, poor, villagers, city dwellers, and landowners, all together at the bridal party. At this event the groom was to prove to the bride's family that he intended to win her love and her hand in marriage by providing them with gifts of goats, food, money, and other, special gifts. There was a lot of goat meat cooked that day. Goat meat is a favorite Kamba dish and is eaten with kashumba, a mixture of sliced chili peppers, tomatoes, cilantro, and onions. Bahati remembers walking through all the people eating, laughing, and celebrating. All of Miriam's sisters were by her side, and though Miriam seemed so nervous, marrying a man whom her father had arranged for her, she was resolute in her decision. There was something admirable in that, Bahati thought. The next scene that came up in Bahati's mind was being at the groom's home. The couple had married. There were tents and everything was lush. It was done upcountry and not in Nairobi where there were skyscrapers and tall hotels. No, this was outside in nature's glorious beauty. The couple came out and danced and shared cake. Then the traditional Kamba dancers came out. Their bodies moved in the air as they performed their acrobatics, tossing each and jolting each other, their skirts swishing in the air and all the dancers moving in rhythm with the drummer. After the performance, the dance floor was opened to others. Many, many speeches from both sets of parents were also given. Bahati and her family left late that night for Nairobi, but an Akamba wedding was well planted in her mind, and a silent expectation was solidified.

Bahati remembers the path that led her to the altar to marry Isamu. She wrestled with her thoughts, her father's wishes, and Mulungu's values. Then she realized Isamu had fought for her. He had shown the world that he loved her. He had overcome racial and cultural differences, he had overcome inner fears of rejection and abandonment, and he had endured Bahati's selfish ambition and strong personality and not given up. Yes, Isamu had fought for Bahati.

She recalled one Thanksgiving when she had planned a lovely dinner for those she loved, but no one showed up. Bahati was distraught, but Isamu came to the rescue. Bahati lived in a gated apartment complex, so it was difficult for those to get in if she did not answer the phone. Isamu was concerned for her. He made his way to her home, which was one hour away from his. He waited until the gate opened, and then he drove in. Bahati heard a knock on the door. Who could it be? It was Isamu. He had scaled the wall and rescued his love from her depression and disappointment. He picked her up and took her to have dinner with his friends. They laughed and played games. But from that time on, it was forever in Bahati's mind that Isamu loved her and would lay his life down for her. Bahati realized that Isamu was rich in what mattered and they would be okay. She stopped worrying about worldly things and focused on becoming the bride Kami-sama had created for Isamu since the beginning of time. Bahati decided to become the woman of noble character that she had learned from her mother and read about in the scriptures. She would let Mulungu (Kami-sama) take her life's experiences and make something beautiful out of them.

Isamu went through his own struggles. He wanted to work, wanted to give more for the wedding, but he knew that the best way he could lead his new bride was to lead her with faith. To do this he would have to leave his heart free for loving Kami-sama and not fill it up with greed and worry. This was hard, because the world has its expectations for a man. From the beginning, Isamu and Bahati had to decide they were not going to be like any ordinary couple. They were going to love each other not for what the other could monetarily give or because they were beautiful people, but because they were going to be friends who loved each other and encouraged each other to trust Kami-sama. They gave each other the things they missed in their youth. And to this day, as husband and wife, they tuck each other in at night and give each other a kiss on the forehead, just as they desired when they were little. The weeds and stones along Life's path make it hard even for the best of us to be perfect. And so, with that love, Isamu and Bahati have grown stronger in their love for each other, Kami-sama, and humanity.

On the wedding day, so many expectations and dreams would be fulfilled. Masako, Bahati's friend, had ordered her a Japanese wedding kimono to surprise Isamu. Masako's mother had come to town before the wedding to teach Bahati how to tie the kimono. Then Masako's husband made a video of Masako and her mother tying the kimono so that Bahati could tie it correctly on her wedding day. There was so much commotion, and so many butterflies in Bahati's stomach, on her wedding day.

"Today I will become a wife," she thought. "Today I will start a new chapter in my life. Today I will leave behind family to unite with Isamu. His people will become my people, and his God, my God. Together we will build up humanity." Bahati decided that she would follow Isamu's lead. She would build him up, and she would lean on the lessons learned from the Ambua women and her mother about loyalty and respect for a husband. And she would seek Kami-sama's guidance throughout her marriage as she had done throughout her youth.

Suddenly the music began, and Bahati walked down the aisle toward Isamu. He was beaming with joy. The elder reminded Isamu to be humble and Bahati to trust, and then they placed the rings on their fingers. They kissed and the elder announced them as husband and wife to the wedding guests. Isamu took Bahati's hand. They walked out toward the crowd and toward tomorrow with the quiet confidence that comes only from living in service to your neighbor and Kami-sama (Mulungu).

Tonight, Bahati listens as Isamu breathes next to her. She found true love and he found her thanks to Kami-sama. No one would have known, though, that Isamu and Bahati would be a couple but Kami-sama. Understanding had hope, Little Brother had vision, and Kami-sama had a plan. Bahati and Isamu just had to seek Him with all their hearts to find that plan. All they had to do was travel over valleys and hills of disbelief to rescue his plan for them and to stand with the courage to embrace it. After they had done all this, they found the everlasting love they had each hoped for. Yes, they found love together and in Kami-sama who always had a plan for Chumvi and Poke. Together, nothing could stop them as long as they clung to Kami-sama and each other, which they did.

VIGNETTE NUMBER EIGHT
The Trails They Paved for Us

Age: man's old friend or foe depending on how you look at it.
"Today I turned another year older in my long life on this earth,"
Bahati thought. "I breathed another breath, embraced Isamu once
more, and received the blessings of my mother. This year I will try
to live a little more thoughtfully, a little more generously, and be
more thankful for my elders, whose trails paved the paths I travel."
Bahati's and Isamu's family's elders and ancestors stood tall, short,
African, Choctaw, Akamba, Caucasian, and Asian in her mind. They
were each of a hard generation that saw poverty and war. Some had
shoes, but many walked barefoot to school and to a better life than
their parents had. Some gave up their dreams for their children,
and for others', their children gave them a better life. But they all
had one thing in common: they knew the value of a life, a breath,
a name, and their time in their Creator's hand.

It had been a long time since Bahati made the long drive to
see Grandma Berry. When she finally got there, her grandma was
sleeping. She thought, "As I sit here looking at Grandma, she looks
so old and worn. I have spent so many days caring about making a
name for myself on this earth, paving a path for my feet to walk, that
I did not notice that my elders and ancestors have paved the paths
that have gotten me this far. My elders' tender hands need to be
held and softened, their voices and stories heard one more time as

the hourglass tilts toward their last breath." Bahati pondered these thoughts quietly as Grandma Berry slept. She thought, "Grandma, I almost missed the most important thing: being here with you in the moment."

Suddenly she heard a voice, "Bahati! Is that you? Have you come to see me?" Bahati's grandmother said.

"Yes, Grandma, I am sorry I stayed away so long. Here, let me hold your hands and sing your favorite song, 'Amazing Grace,'" Bahati says to her grandmother. As Bahati sings, she stares deeply into the chocolate brown eyes of her grandmother that have now turned blue with age. She sees the woman who lived through the Depression in the southern part of the United States as an African American child. She sees the woman who endured racism and prejudice, but did not let that stop her from working, putting her children through college, and helping others. Yes, as Bahati sang, she thought, "This is where I need to be, beside this woman if only for a moment, to comfort her and hear her tell her stories one last time."

Grandma Berry grew up poor in the South. It was hard for her as a child. She told Bahati once that they did not have shoes. She attended a few years of elementary school and then had to stop so she could work. She was determined, though, to learn how to write and read, so after she married and her children grew up, she went to night school and became literate. Her letters to Bahati and her family over the years were her testimony to her writing ability and freedom to express herself in ink. Grandma Berry loved her Bible and read it every morning before she went to work. She read it until she could not see anymore. Now, when Bahati comes to visit her, she reads her some of her favorite verses. Grandma was very generous, yet sometimes stingy. It took time for Bahati to understand that her grandmother wanted her to learn how to work and make it on her own. She knew the world was cruel and hard. Bahati reflected that perhaps her grandmother was torn between not giving anything and giving too much. Bahati knew deep inside she mostly wanted to share her faith and hope and have relationships with all of her children and grandchildren. Bahati thought Grandma grew more and more lonely as the years passed and her friends died. Bahati pondered, "I learned from Grandma that money does not replace a solid friendship or relationship with someone. I can buy them things, but it won't make up for my inability to talk or listen when they need a listening ear."

Bahati noticed the characteristic of conserving was not limited to Grandma Berry. Bahati's father, who had been born into humble beginnings, was also big on conserving. Sometimes it got down to how much water was in a glass. Her father had seen many famines, and her grandmother had had to live sparingly through the Depression. Bahati's father and Grandma Berry each had a different story, but similar behavior, and yet this was a path they paved for Bahati and her siblings. Bahati thought to herself, "They taught me how to conserve my money." Bahati did not have much, however, and sometimes feared not having enough to share with everyone. Bahati realized, as she grew older, that being selfish and hoarding money didn't do any good, and neither did enabling people. She had come to see that money was used interchangeably with love in the world. However, unlike love, money had a limit. Love did not. She learned, over time, that love did not harm its neighbor. A person never needed too much or too little love. They just needed to be loved. Bahati remembered the parable about the rich man who boasted about all the money he had and then died the same night, taking nothing with him. The man in the parable had great treasures and food to spare, but he did not want to share with anyone else. He boasted that he was planning to fly to Paris, London, and Shanghai to make his business deals, but on the way to the airport, his car crashed and he was no more. Bahati could relate to this man, as she liked to hoard her riches for herself. Bahati desired so much to be a loving neighbor, but the greed in her heart and desire for nice things always distracted her from special moments like being with Grandma Berry, holding her hands, and singing with her. "These special moments cannot be purchased," Bahati thought to herself, and yet they cost something to make them happen. "It's worth it!" Bahati thought as she smiled back into her grandmother's eyes.

The sun was starting to set, as it was a winter month when Bahati had come to visit her grandmother. But Bahati did not want to leave her grandmother; she had been away for so long, and for what? Nothing—work on the weekends. That could wait, no more putting work before family, love, or Kami-sama.

"How are you doing?" Grandma asked. "Are you working? What do you do?"

"I teach," Bahati replied.

"Do you teach boys or girls? Who are the smarter ones, the boys or the girls?" Grandma asked. Again, this was a generational question. It came from a woman who grew up in a time when boys were valued over girls, men over women, and then World War II came and women went to work. Women and men discovered that women were industrious and could work beyond bearing children and cooking and cleaning up the house. Bahati realized as she looked at her grandmother that not every God-created woman was considered a woman before the civil rights movement, and Grandma had many scars from that harsh reality. She'd spent many days cleaning up after people for not a lot of money. Bahati gave her answer slowly, "They are all talented, Grandma." Which is what Bahati believed, as she was a great fan of the work of Dr. Howard Gardner, which says we all have a talent, we all have something to share and to give the other—the blind, deaf, mute, and lame too. Just look at Helen Keller, a story worth telling over and over again to those who are willing to listen and learn from it. Bahati continued, "Grandma, they are all talented. They each have a special and unique way of learning. They teach me how to be a better teacher. I cannot teach them all in the same way. They won't learn if I do. Some learn by listening, others by looking, others by touching, still others by perceiving. Some need to be left alone and others need someone nearby to learn with, from, and sometimes even teach. Yes, Grandma, each of my students is different, and they need a different teacher each year."

"Mmm, teaching, learning. Do you like teaching, Bahati?" Grandma asked.

"Sometimes I do and sometimes I don't. Being a good teacher to all my students is a lot of work, and it is hard because teachers are not appreciated."

"Mmm, but we do what we do because it's good, not because we will get a thank-you," Grandma told Bahati.

"Oh, Grandma, that is hard a lesson to learn."

"It is hard to teach, too, Bahati. 'God don't mean no harm,'" Grandma Berry's favorite phrase. Grandma Berry went on, "Sometimes he has to teach us to trust him, so we will last awhile longer on this earth and not fall down from all the injustices. Two wrongs don't make a right, you know. God is not going to teach you a hard lesson and let you down. He'll catch you just when you are about to quit and give you eagles' wings, just like it says in the book of Isaiah." Bahati smiled at Grandma and embraced her wisdom.

Bahati pondered awhile on what her grandmother had said. Then she saw it clear as day. God had let her grandmother pave a road for Bahati to walk in faith through life's trials. She could believe in Mulungu because her Grandmother Berry and Susu both loved God despite the challenges life threw them. Grandma Berry, a black woman living in the South facing racism and poverty, had a dream for an education to read and write but had to wait until her children graduated college. Susu, poor and humble, had to live through many famines. Bahati thought and waited. Patience in the face of suffering; Grandma Berry and Susu had paved the road for Bahati to face suffering with patience. What a gift! If only Bahati would cherish it and hold it dear to her heart like it was worth a six-figure job. It might let her walk just a few more steps with contentment in her heart rather than bitter envy for what she did not have.

"Grandma, let me hold your other hand," Bahati whispered as her grandmother started to grow tired. Bahati sat a little while longer with her grandmother. She pondered her Choctaw grandfather who was half Caucasian and whom she had never met, grandmother's husband. He had died before Bahati was born. She knew very little about him except that he was a construction worker and that he built the house his family lived in with his own hands. He was a strong man with a brave heart, choosing a dark woman when everyone preferred a lighter one. And yet, not just choosing this woman, but loving her at a time when it was not popular, when he could have chosen anyone. He chose Grandma Berry. Even though he could go into white-only restaurants when his daughter and wife could not, he married her anyway, and took the mark that the world so desperately wants to blame God for: prejudice. Yet the world does not realize that after the resurrection, any curse was gone for good through the blood of the lamb. But legalism often blinds us, it blinds the best and the worst of us. Everyone marching in justice's name, except Justice is not marching with us. Grandfather paved the road of diversity for Bahati. He showed her that you could love someone different from yourself. You can love them even if it means someone else won't like you for it, because love covers over hate.

Sometimes Bahati thought Isamu reminded her of grandfather. Bahati, too, was always curious about diversity. She thought love was one way to break down the barriers. She recalled a picture she had drawn as a young adolescent. It was a picture of a young boy and girl on a date. Bahati was always enthralled by courtship. The picture was unique though, because it was collage of a diverse couple. Just as she had used many pieces of paper to make this picture, Mulungu had patched many stories in Isamu and Bahati's life to form one diverse, unique, and beautiful story. When Bahati got home that night, she pulled out her old picture, which she kept with her artwork and other childhood treasures, and showed it to Isamu. Curious, Isamu admitted that he had always wanted to marry a dark woman

Bahati's Multicultural Dream

like Bahati. They laughed together as Mulungu had given them the desires of their hearts.

Bahati thought, "My elders, my ancestors, they all paved a road for me to travel. If only I will stay on the narrow road they have paved for me, if only I will take their faith and grasp it as my own. Their brave faith, love for love itself, walking with grace under fire, and most of all loving their enemies. These steppingstones they've laid help guide the way to a more content life. A more quiet life!"

Her grandmother was just about asleep. Bahati got up to leave, here grandmother said, "Are you going, Bahati?"

"Well, it is just about time, but I will sit just a little while longer." Bahati closed her eyes for a while and thought back to her Umau. Umau lived in Kibwezi all his life. She remembered that he knew how to make a sling shot out of twigs, and showed Mutuku and her how to make one on a visit he made to the house in Moi Estate.

"He loved my father," Bahati thought. "My father did not always see this, but Umau loved him, cherished him, and was proud of him." His son, educated in an American university and a landowner, his son whom his wife bore in Kibwezi where they had little water and sometimes little food, his son who had beat the odds. Umau was in a constant state of celebration.

Umau was part Akamba and part Arab. Kibwezi was very close to the coastal region where the Swahili people lived. The Swahili people were a mixture of Bantus and Arabs who had come to the coastal area to trade ivory, gold, servants, and other precious things. They had done this for generations prior to the Portuguese and Vasco da Gama's conquests and discoveries. Umau was truly an Ambua man from Kibwezi. And in her mind, Bahati could see his yellow-brown skin, high cheekbones, smooth, silky hair, and his big smile. In that moment she thought that Umau had paved the road for a long ancestral tree that if she had the time and energy, she would one day return, chart, and find. He gave her a sense of belonging to history, to something that, though humble, was rich with human life, recorded in the soil of Kibwezi and flowing down the Tana River into the Indian Ocean. Yes! Bahati had a long ancestral history from which to draw her humanity. She had also Umau's generous smile and joy for life, even though he had to walk miles to the Mombasa Highway to catch a matatu to Nairobi, and then another to Lang'ata, and then walk down Mukoma Road with his aged legs and walking stick, all so he could see his son and smile at him. Yes! Smile, just smile. Even though the matatu rides were long and squishy with everyone jammed into together, and though the walk was long for an older man, Umau still came to see his son. He loved his son and would do anything to come by the house to see him, the family, and the children.

Bahati could hear her grandmother breathing deeply. The sun had set and Bahati put her grandmother's hand on top of the other one, kissed her grandmother on the forehead, and walked away silently into the night air. As Bahati walked up the street to her car, she thought, "It has been a long time since I saw grandmother." Bahati promised herself it would not be that long again. She got in her car and drove away with a refreshed heart and a clear reminder that we all reap what we sow. Bahati decided to sow love and relationships over greed and getting ahead, but it would be a battle to overcome the tide around her, racing forward, yet going nowhere.

As Bahati drove home that night, she thought of the other elders Mulungu had sent her. Her thoughts fell on two in particular: her mentors Fred and Susan. Fred had taken Bahati on as a young teacher and mentored her, and Susan had helped Bahati become healthy and strong inside. As she passed the streetlights and merged onto the freeway, she reflected on all that Fred and Susan had endured for her. They were Scottish and Jewish. Bahati knew that they both stood for equality, but she did not realize the extent of this until she actually left their establishments and was on her own in the world. On her own, she faced the racial slurs, disrespect and disregard for her hard work, and accusations for her good deeds. They stung and cut deep. At times Bahati felt she could not go on anymore. But as she drove home that night, she started to cry because she realized that, for many years, Fred and Susan had shielded her from the false accusations, the racial slurs, the harsh disregard, and the outright disrespect towards her. And as the tears moved down her face, Bahati realized how much Fred and Susan had done for her as a young professional: they gave her the freedom to work with confidence, with no glass ceiling, just love to give. But there was a cost all the time, and Fred and Susan took this quietly on themselves so Bahati could grow. Mulungu gave Bahati a chance to breathe and know that she could do anything because the glass ceiling was coming and Bahati would need all her elders to help her break through. Bahati was almost home. She wiped the snot from her nose with her sleeve. She realized that she too could pave a path. A path of gratitude for the Freds and Susans in her life who took a silent beating—even though they were white-skinned and not brown like her—so she could go forward. Bahati drove into her parking space at her house. Hatred is not the color of our skin, it really is the condition of our hearts. And, in that moment, Bahati could understand why Yesu said, "Forgive them, Father, they know not what they do." Bahati thought, "We really don't know what we do, but when we do, we must chose to forgive, love, and go on. I must chose to breathe Mulungu's air, Kami-sama's promise, God's love, and let Life take one hand and Isamu the other, and let them lead me down the narrow road." Bahati promised herself that she, too, would give up her life to pave a road with Isamu for those needing help back onto the road of compassion. Bahati got out of the car, closed the door, and made her way to her house, where Isamu was waiting with a hot meal from their favorite Japanese restaurant.

Isamu and Bahati did many things together and enjoyed each other's company. Isamu and Bahati especially appreciated their trips to the beach. They had a favorite Victorian inn they would stay at when they got away from the hustle and bustle of the city. It was a short mile into town and a small distance from the beach. Once at the beach, they would stand on the cliffs and watch the ocean waves crash with great force. The ocean was different all around the world. Bahati had the opportunity to wade in the warm, crystal-clear Indian Ocean as a child and walk along the chilly Pacific Ocean as a young adult. She was moved by the Baltic Sea as she stood on its edge with her childhood friend so many years ago. Water and Bahati always seemed to go together—water soothed her soul and comforted her. As a young adolescent, it was her walks by the river. As an adult, it was her walks by the ocean. On one of their visits to the Victorian inn, Isamu told her stories of his childhood, elders, and ancestors. He told her of their suffering, joy, honor, and lives. He spoke highly of one elder in particular who shared stories with him about his ancestors. This elder had lived through World War II and endured the marks of the war. In another account, Isamu told Bahati how another one of his elders who had been asked to fight in WWII but, after Pearl Harbor, he was not allowed to enlist again. He was deeply wounded inside.

Fear, prejudice, and the Japanese internment camps had left a deep scar in his heart.

Prior to the war, some of his elders, though not rich in material things, were rich in zest and spirit of life. One elder in particular told him how she walked barefoot through the fields in the morning to learn Japanese prior to running to her American middle school. Her American teachers advocated for her. Teachers can change the course of a child's life. Father Patrick had changed Bahati's father. Isamu told Bahati how the teachers of this elder asked her family to allow her to continue to middle school. The parents agreed. The elder did not stop there but went on to high school and college. This elder, later, was so grateful for her teacher's kindness and persistence.

In another account, Isamu shared about how his elders, though they had great zest for life, still faced racism in their careers. One elder was a registered nurse, but she had to initially work as an assistant because only the Caucasian nurses were allowed to be lead nurses. Isamu shared that Asians were the assistants and the people native to the land were the cleaners. With time, however, this elder did become a registered nurse. As Isamu told Bahati this story it resonated for her: the glass ceiling.

As a young undergraduate student, and before she married, Bahati had taken an Asian American course. It was then that she learned about the struggles of Asian Americans, including Japanese Americans. She later read *The Accidental Asian* by Eric Liu and was struck by the silent oppression many Asians endure. It was in and during this class that she learned about the glass ceiling and began to notice the number of aged Asian people who rode the bus during the day in the city. They were educated but could only go so far in their careers. After she married Isamu, she started to learn more and hear the stories of the Japanese, not only in America but in Japan, too.

Isamu was skilled in martial arts and had the heart of an ancient samurai. He had strong Japanese honor in his heart and was the kind of person who would fall on his sword for his friend. Such character you rarely see up close, but Bahati loved Isamu and loved that he taught her the Japanese way. She met also Masako who taught her a lot about Japanese women, before she married Isamu. Masako came into Bahati's life when the cherry tree bloomed and Isamu asked Bahati to be his girlfriend. Masako taught her how to make sushi and miso soup. In turn, Bahati befriended Masako and helped her encourage the other Japanese women who had come to America with their husbands but were socially isolated because they did not speak a lot of English. Like DNA, Isamu and Bahati's lives were woven together through different prior life experiences, so when they met, they could appreciate each other's uniqueness.

Bahati took note as she met Isamu's elders after they were married. Bahati thought to herself, "How did they endure such inequality?" Bahati had felt the impact of the glass ceiling, too. Isamu's elders were beautiful and industrious people, gentle and compassionate. Then she realized that Isamu's elders had paved the way for Isamu and her to walk in an unfair world, to have compassion in suffering, to find purpose when there is none, to make something from nothing, and to keep it for the next generation and the ones after that. On one trip to visit Isamu's elders, Bahati remembered the kind words said to her and Isamu. "Love each other, be good to each other, and hold onto each other." Those words were not said just to make warm, fuzzy feelings; the elder was paving a road for them to travel. Stick close together and love each other. If you do, then nothing will stop you.

Bahati pondered, "Am I grateful for our ancestors, our elders, and the trails they paved for us all?" Bahati thought, "We shuffle our feet as though shackled together. Got to keep moving. Can't stop or someone else will to take my place. Someone else will take my dream. Perhaps someday we will appreciate the lives of our elders that light the way for us and tell their stories to generations to come. A lost voice it seems, our ancestors." Bahati reasoned to herself, "My place, my hope, my dream, my life; they can all be taken from me. But the trails I will pave for those after me, and the story my life will tell, the truth of who I was, the time I lived in, and the breath

I breathed. These cannot be taken from me. It can only be given as it was given freely." Bahati realized that she had to let go of her human gods that she so much wanted approval from. Instead she must love people and recognize that they are broken, just like her, even if they deny it and demand dominion over her. She must trust Kami-sama, and not fear the angry man, the hateful man, the unkind woman, her own resentment, her own pride, or her own fear. She must walk in the path of her elders and ancestors and pave a trail worth remembering. She must learn to receive and give compassion, for we all need it to live.

Bahati, now quiet and peaceful inside, felt one more set of elders and ancestors calling at her to listen to their life stories. They were Bahati's elders and ancestors of hope. Mrs. Young was a woman of faith, an African American, and a teacher. She mentored Bahati, when Bahati graduated from college and began working. Bahati recalled over the years the deep talks Mrs. Young and her would have about life, faith, and education. Mrs. Young had even come to Bahati's engagement party and wedding. Now Mrs. Young was very old and in her 80s. She still looked as young as she had when Bahati first met her, but she moved a little slower. Mrs. Young had dark chocolate brown skin, a brilliant laugh, and always dressed herself in the finest clothes. Mrs. Young knew her history and her God well. One day, Bahati came over to visit her. That day, Mrs. Young reminded Bahati of people throughout human history who faced the harsh facts that the impossible could be done, despite the odds. She spoke of Abraham and how his confidence was rewarded with virtue. She shared how Abraham's unwavering courage opened up the door for the trail of truth, life, and love for all. She shared how slaves throughout history had emulated this faith. Bahati learned from Mrs. Young that day that human history cannot be forgotten. Mrs. Young implored Bahati to write and tell the truth of the historical accounts that happen in our human story, both pleasant and painful. Like Abraham, Bahati could choose to hope for the impossible: a common humanity not bound by their fears of each other's differences. It is because of this great hope that Bahati realized she did not have to fear those who oppress her or oppress those she fears, but she could overcome fear with compassion and understanding. In a quiet moment Bahati looked up, and saw her soul illuminating through her facial expressions in the mirror hanging on the wall. She sensed the scars in her soul that she had made from choosing revenge over compassion. Bahati pondered the compassion she had received from other people and Mulungu. She decided to forgive and keep forgiving as revenge had only bruised her soul. Mulungu continuously shows compassion, which brings life to the soul. Bahati realized that the road had been ignited for her, so that with time, grace, and truth through human-compassion her heart would heal. Compassion and hope had saved the hour. If only we would choose them," Bahati thought to herself. Bahati realized that difference did not have to be feared, and love could conquer fear in the souls of men. And, with that, Bahati smiled to herself and picked up her chopsticks to eat her sushi and teriyaki chicken. Isamu said, "Together with Kami-sama, Bahati, nothing can stop us." Bahati thought to herself, Kami-sama has given Isamu and me a chance to do the impossible. Two unique and different lives from two different corners of the earth have crossed to create one common life with a common story. A story that can help those who listen find their own voice among the pages, perhaps hear their own story among the stories, and live to tell their own story to the next generation!

A Story Is Told

People will know Compassion
Inspired by Love!
All of you be one in mind
and feeling; love as (family);
and be compassionate!
1Peter 3:8 (CJV)

The END

A Note to Classroom Teachers from the Author

Shiffman (2010) discusses the challenges experienced by teachers and students in the multicultural classroom. There are insufficient multicultural literary works available to children of all races. The limited expanse of tools available to address multicultural issues presented in literature and the classroom often dismay children and teachers. Caucasian children are sometimes faced with the harsh realities of their ancestors' attitudes and actions toward people of color. Some are overwhelmed and respond defensively, while others attempt to embrace the truth and promote change. Bi-racial, bi-cultural, Asian, Latino, Native American, African, and African American are no different than Caucasian children. Even worse for students of color is listening to repeated stories of cultural defeat. These stories leave students of color dismayed and sometimes disinterested in the literature available to them.

In the African and African American communities, oral literature has strong cultural relevance. Faith, elders, and community provide an avenue for this oral culture to continue on to the next generation. As the urban city continues to grow and families become more and more fragmented, the opportunity for hearing ancestral and world stories is lost. As a result, children are left to textbooks and literature to hear the stories of the past and present. It is important that these stories reflect and communicate hope for the young reader living in the urban community. Stories, poems, fiction, and non-fiction prose play an important role in letting the next generation know about life and what it has to offer them. Throughout history, literature softens the soul. It provides expression and relief from the harsh realities that the soul must endure. It is therefore essential that all children be able to access literature as a form of inspiration.

Hughes-Hassel and Rodge (2007) describe the challenges faced by many adolescents from urban communities. Reading for pleasure is not an activity many of these children seek due to their inadequate reading skills. It is even harder when the literature available to them does not reflect their culture or inspire them through life. Critical Race Theory (CRT) has been applied to concepts and content taught in children's literature for even the youngest of children (Hughes-Hassel & Cox, 2010). When applied to the breadth of current children's literature, principals of CRT, including racism, counter-storytelling, and Interest Convergence Theory (ICT), expose the need for continued growth and development. Globalization has brought multicultural literature to a new level. Children learn about the world's people through the lens of literature and the media. ICT has a significant role in what each nation teaches its children about the other. Without it, prejudices and fears remain and our world does not reach its full potential.

Multicultural literature, when done well, provides a chance for healing. Shiffman (2010) discusses multiculturalism and how it is coming of age in literature through a variety of avenues, including intergenerational stories. He describes the work of three unique authors: Yezierska, Cisneros, and Tan. These authors and many others, including Hughes, Jacobs, and Naidoo, address the current experiences of many children of color living in the twenty-first century. A continued need in children's literature is African books authored by Africans who know the stories of their people (Osaki, 2004). Given the dearth of African authors, many stereotypes about African people continue, and the prejudices of colonialism are silently solidified in the hearts of the next generation. *The Trails I Walked at the Foot of Ngong Hills* captures intergenerational relationships and experiences in a Mukamba and African American girl who lived in

Kenya and later married into the Asian American culture. It captures, for the next generation, a twenty-first century multicultural story. The monograph in this text provides the scholarly vignette on the topic of multicultural children's literature. It follows the story and provides teachers an understanding of the text to allow them to assist students in exploring the story in greater depth. The monograph and glossary are written to help the instructor, support the young reader to understand the different metaphors and historical information, as well as analyze the poetry. The authors cited in this monograph have compelling and current multicultural stories to assist the teacher in creating a genre of multicultural literature in the classroom. Hence, providing students some non-conventional literature that deals with the issues of culture, race, and diversity. *The Trails I Walked at the Foot of Ngong Hills* was written to offer hope for a better tomorrow through the Bahati's bi-cultural journey as a Mukamba and African American person. Bahati shares her experiences with faith, elders, and humanity, and follows in the footsteps of her Kamba heritage. Akamba value Mulungu, elders, and the human family. *The Trails I Walked at the Foot of Ngong Hills* is a scholarly young readers' book, designed to help young readers find their own voice in a multi-cultural world.

References

Hughes-Hassell, S., & Cox, E. J. (2010). Inside board books: Representations of people of color. *The Library Quarterly, 80(3),* 211-230.

Hughes-Hassel, S. and Rodge, P. (2007). The leisure reading habits of urban adolescents. *Journal of Adolescent and Adult Literacy,* 51:1, 22-33

Mbiti, J. S. (Ed) (1984). *Akamba Stories, The Oxford Library of African Literature.* Nairobi: Oxford University Press

Osaki, L. T. (2003). African Children's Literature: a scholar's guide. *University of Dar es Salaam Library Journal, 5(1). 67-79.*

Shiffman. D. (2010). Mapping intergenerational tension in multicultural coming-of-age literature. *Multicultural Perspectives, 12, 1, 29-33.*

Glossary

Kamba/Swahili Language	Japanese Language	Hawaiian Language	English Language
A Levels			General Certificate of Education: The Advanced Level
Amani			Peace
Akamba			Plural for Kamba. Kamba people
Ambua			Kamba Clan
Bantu			Some East, South, and Middle Africans of the Bantu linguistic and ethnic group
Chumvi			Salt
Form			High School Grade
Harambee			Synergy
	Isamu		Courage
Jamuri			Independence
Kamba			Bantu tribe
Kashumba			Dipping sauce
Kibwezi			Kamba town
Kikuyu			Bantu tribe
Lang'ata			Nairobi suburb
Lake Nyanza			Lake Victoria
Machakos			Capitol of the Eastern Province of Kenya
Matatu			Privately Owned Minibus

Kamba/Swahili Language	Japanese Language	Hawaiian Language	English Language
Maziwa Lala			Fermented milk
Mbeni			Kamba dance/drums
Mombasa			Kenyan Coastal City
Mukamba			Kamba Person
Mulungu	Kami-sama		God
Ngoma			Drums
Ngong Hills			Ridge Peaks along the Rift Valley
'O' Levels			General Certificate of Education: The Ordinary Level
		Poke	Fish
Primary School			Elementary School
Raffia			Shiny hair string
River Tana			Longest River in Kenya
Secondary School			High School
Shilling			Kenyan Currency
Standards			Grades
Swahili			East African Language
Sukari guru			Unprocessed sugar
Susu			Grandmother
Ugali			A dish cooked with maize meal to a doughlike consistency
Uji			Porridge
Ukambani			The Land of the Kamba People
Umau			Grandfather
Yesu			Jesus

Author:
Dr. Martina Kaumbulu Ebesugawa

Dr. Ebesugawa is an adjunct professor of Child Development and Education at De Anza College and two other colleges in the San Francisco Bay Area. She holds a doctorate in Learning and Instruction and an MA in Early Childhood Special Education. Dr. Ebesugawa is bi-cultural, born to a Kenyan father and African American mother. She was born in the United States of America and grew up in Nairobi, Kenya. She later returned to the United States of America where she attended college and married. She brings a unique and authentic multicultural perspective to her work in the field of early childhood education. She learns something new from her students each year. She understands the complexities of human differences, but she greatly appreciates the potential of the human spirit towards compassion. Lastly, she enjoys inspiring her students to become the future inventors, entrepreneurs, and educators of their generation.

Illustrator:
Juan J. Marquez Portal

Juan was born in the city of Lima, Peru. His grandfather, Don Luis Portal, was a great painter, and motivated Juan to become an artist. He learned various techniques of drawing and painting, making his early presentation when he was nine years old. An oil painting reflecting the Peruvian Amazon, and the admiration of his family, gave him even more determination to explore the arts.

Juan studied at San Agustin School in Lima, Peru. Over the years, Juan participated as a graphic designer juror in a class at the Peruvian Publicity Institute. He taught also semantics in the Montessori Peruvian Art Academy. Today, Juan works with great enthusiasm, joy, and amazing talent on each of his projects. He diligently works to capture powerful emotions and expressions on canvas and the computer screen.

CPSIA information can be obtained
at www.ICGtesting.com
Printed in the USA
LVIC07n1428090913
351651LV00027B